After Dead

Terrance Wolfe

Contents

Prologue

I died, few months back from a car accident. You must be wondering why I'm still here telling you all this. Well, I have a theory. If I could write my story in the hereafter, then I could find a way to send a message to the other side and tell them where I was... I could let my family know my whereabouts and tell everyone else that the world of the dead is not the place that they've read from any religious and spiritual books. You've been fooled by those writers. All of you. You could ask for a refund if you wanted to but that isn't the reason why I'm writing... Consider this as a warning. You could thank me later, but I wanted you to hear my words: You're all in grave danger.

Chapter 1

How did I end up dead? The last thing I remember was driving my mini Suzuki car that was given to me by my father as a birthday present when I turned 16. It was the first day of my junior year and I was on my way to school that morning feeling excited. Rose, my red mini swift car as I called it, was moving at normal speed on the highway. I knew that the road was wet because of the rain this morning but there was no other car behind me and I was eager to get to school to see my friend Martin. I climbed to bed early last night, but my brother Ram was playing a video game in his room, and the explosive sound on the background was literally banging my wall preventing me from dozing off. I was awake until midnight but eventually my body gave up and surrendered to tiredness. You couldn't blame me; I was running late. I didn't notice that I was almost at the crossing or it must have slipped my mind. A Rihanna song was blaring inside my car and it was my favorite one. I'm not really a good singer but good enough to sing along with it and that was literally what I was doing when it happened. Before I reached the intersection, I saw the traffic light wasn't working but it was early, and I didn't anticipate a huge truck coming in from the left side with a driver thinking the same thing that I was. I know it was reckless driving; both the truck driver and I were guilty of that. The tragedy happened in a blink of an eye. The front of the truck was coming in so fast that I didn't get the chance to scream. My voice cowered behind my throat and all I could do was stare at the humongous vehicle before it collided on my car and killed me.

But before I lost my consciousness, I was suddenly hit with flashbacks from the events in my life. It bolted like a moving train and I had no control over it. I saw myself when I was a girl in a swing at a playground and my mom was pushing me from the back while my dad was standing nearby watching us. Both were laughing and I was laughing too. I could almost hear their laughter. It was before my parents got separated. We were happy back then. Then the scene changed. I was sitting beside my mom on the bed while she was cradling my baby brother in her arms. We were in the master bedroom, the sun sipped through the window bathing the room with light. I could feel my mother's joy as she played with my brother and then she looked at me and reached a hand to caress my face. She smiled and her face was radiant and beautiful. The feeling of happiness I felt was immediate, it surged through my spine and made me giggled. My mom was amused by this and her smiles widened as she moved closer to kiss my forehead. Then there was my brother Ram when he was a toddler, we were playing in the living room while our parents were on the couch watching over us. My brother was dancing awkwardly without music and all of us clapping our hands encouraging him to go on. Those were happy memories, all of it. I anticipated seeing more but then there was nothing. The movie was cut short, a total blackout. I was dead.

By then I realized how short life was, it could be taken anytime without a warning. I didn't have a warning when my time came, and I didn't have a say over it. Death will happen anytime no matter what. It doesn't matter if you're young or healthy, able or not. All of us will have our chance with death, the only question is when. Unfortunately for me I got my answer first. There was no sign for the candidates. For instance, I couldn't say that my short life on earth was perfect, but it wasn't that bad either. My father Andrew and my mother Mercy were amazing parents. They raised my brother Ram and me the best way they knew how, and I didn't have any complaints over that. They got separated when I was ten, but they were best friends and dad visited us during weekends. My father worked hard to provide for the family even if he lived in a flat along downtown near to his office. He's a lawyer. My mother stayed at home to take good care with our needs. She was perfect. But because of her complicated status with my dad, she decided to scan the local newspaper one day looking for a job. Gladly, she got one in the nursing home taking care of the elderly. She loved going to work every day and I could see that she was happy with it. She must have missed the act of waking up early in the morning, tearing through the morning rush to avoid getting late. Working kept her balance.

My brother and I quarreled most of the time. He was doing prank jokes at me the moment he pronounced the word P-R-A-N-K. I wanted to strangle him every time I saw him but that didn't mean that we hated each other. I guessed that was normal for siblings. I loved my brother so much; sometimes he was just so irritating. So, it was a shock that death gave me a gate pass first to ghost town whereas the percentage of criminals roaming around town was over the top. Why didn't death prioritize those types of people instead of me? Why me? Well, too late to whine about it now because whether I like it or not, having a pulse was no longer an option for me anymore. I was freakin' dead.

A weekend before my accident, Martin Frey, my gay best friend was blowing the hoot out of his metallic blue mini cooper in front of our house. We decided to see each other and enjoyed what's left of the summer before we plunged into junior high. I told my mom that I would come home before dinner as I walked past her in the living room. She was busy changing the drapery and I didn't wait for her to turn around. I stormed out of the house sprinting to where Martin parked his luxury car. I hopped inside the car to see Martin greeting me with all smiles. He was rocking a perfectly tanned skin from his summer vacation in Brazil. It looked great on him, with his surfer blonde hair and icy blue eyes –he reminded me of a Ken doll. Of course, that's a complement for Martin. He's loaded alright, both of his parents were into business and they're rich as hell. But I didn't envy him because the downside of having rich parents was, they were never there for him. They would always pay someone to look after him because they were too busy travelling the world. I pitied Martin sometimes, imagined growing up alone with nothing but the household help. But probably that was the reason why we're besties, because of how Martin hated his family, it was even ridiculous. Besides, he made me laugh so loud I couldn't even care.

"Hey there Ms. Goods!" Martin greeted me with his breathy voice.

"Frey! Welcome back." I greeted him with a smile.

"You look so..."

"Tanned?" He interrupted. "Well, life is a beach in Rio, Brah-zil." Said Martin in ultra-exaggeration while flailing a hand in the air.

" bee-aa-cchh?" I asked, teasing.

"Yes, bitch!" He said and we laughed together like we always did.

Laughing was so easy every time the fabulous Frey was around. I couldn't let the grin out of my face. I had to admit that I missed having him with me because the past two weeks being alone, it was already too much for me to bear - I was bored to death. My brother Ram was out with his friends most of the time and I was the loser who didn't have a group of friends beside Martin. He was my only close friend. We drove off along River Gate Avenue and emerged on the Highway. Martin maneuvered the chic car and turned right; he then rolled the front windows down to enjoy the afternoon breeze. The air was warm on my face, my hair was flying over at my back and I let it because it felt great. The sun was starting to set, and the sky burned flamingo from afar. I could still see some of the houses from the River Gate and those that were along the highway as well. Most establishments along the road were situated a few yards apart from each other and there were cars outside. We were on our way to Barry's Diner to try their new burritos. The Diner was located downtown, and it was easy to find. Or you could just ask anyone around town, and they'll point you where it was. Almost all the students from school hung out at Barry's during weekends. The food was okay, but it was affordable and there were at least three billiard tables at the back, a flat screen that played mainly sport channels and the bar area played a good selection of upbeat music. It was a destination to go to with friends and meet people our age. Silent Hills was a small quaint town in the state of Mississippi. There's nothing much happening here if you're looking for something big. We had the Border Mall overlooking the beach where most of the coffee shops were located. Next to it was the amusement park with a boardwalk to the coastline if you're the type who enjoys bon fire or a walk along seaside. The Gulf Coast was splendid during the afternoon and family cars piled up on the driveway to have ice cream or hotdogs and mallows. In downtown we had Jerry's Grocery Store from which you could buy almost anything you needed in the food department. There were few small establishments selling different stuff and services like shoe repair and plumbing. A high-end restaurant in Greek revival façade was located two blocks from the city hall. The only church devoted to Saint Augustine was run by a new ordained priest, Father Jess Bradley. He used to teach at Silent Hills High before he became the director of the Church, that's how I knew him.

We arrived at Barry's and I was excited to see that the place was filled with people. Martin drove the car slowly as we navigated the parking lot to find our spot. It was full and we were lucky enough to find our space at the far end. It wasn't the best spot, but we didn't have options to complain either.

"We have a full house." Martin said smiling.

"I guess everybody is here" I giggled.

"It'll be fun!" He was excited too.

We parked the car and got out. Before we headed to the Diner, Martin turned to face me, his eyes beaming.

"How do I look?" He turned around to showcase his outfit.

"Like you just got out of Teen Vogue?" I said.

"Thank you! And you from Seventeen Mag." We giggled and started to walk hand in hand to Barry's.

Martin entered the diner like he owned the place and I was trailing behind him like an assistant. He looked so colorful with his pastel pink button down and apple green short ensemble. I was practically right; everybody was at Barry's. It seemed like the party was in full swing and the music was literally blasting that made the whole diner pulsate. I realized that it was Saturday and probably the reason why everyone felt obligated to go out because it was the last day to enjoy the vacation. Classes would start on Monday. Most of the people were standing with a bottle of beer in hand; the ones sitting on tables were busy updating each other about what they did the entire summer. I heard Jessa King just got back from a summer vacation in Paris with her family, Martha's fun outback experience in Australia etc. The girls were gossiping about it and it was all over twitter as well. Poor little Lola Goods, whose last name was not privileged enough to own a huge house in Zion Road where Martin and all other rich families lived. Sometimes it sucked to be me. Though River Gate wasn't that bad, it was where the middle-class families from Silent Hills resided. I had to give that to my parents that we didn't end up living along Parade Loop which was literally where the trailer park homes. But I didn't have anything against people who lived there because most of them were hard working individuals who just wanted to make ends meet, some of them I knew from school. Meryl was one of them. She was a scholar, a tiny brown-haired girl who sat beside me during English class and worked a few hours selling ice cream at the boardwalk after last period. I respected her for that, I know it was hard for her, but she managed to balance work and studies at the same time. She also managed to stay anonymous at school; I understood that she preferred to stay in the corner to avoid picking from other students. Especially those girls who loved to call themselves popular. Yeah, there were few of them at Silent Hills High and unluckily I wasn't one of them. Not that I desired to be one – spending each day with Martin made me realize that being popular was stressful. Having a life under a microscope? Not my thing. I didn't mind being anonymous like Meryl, it was a choice though. I could do the things that I like doing without anyone noticing and criticizing me. But I could dream about being nameless... not when the most popular guy in school asked you out on a date, because girls would instantly hate you and suddenly, you'll be enemy number one.

Gossip literally travels at the speed of light – that's tried and tested. My infamous ascension from being unknown to the highly abhorred person by the female species of Silent Hills High happened last semester, a few weeks before finals. Since our last class normally ended early during Friday, Martin held my wrist and literally dragged me to the Soccer Field to watch the school team practice. SHH chose Eagle as the school symbol and the soccer team automatically picked it up as the team's name and called themselves as The Eagles. The team practiced three times a week and that was MWF, which was the number of times my good old friend Martin dragged me to the field to watch them practice. When I asked him about it, he shrugged and said he loved watching the game. I knew for a fact that he knew nothing about soccer and so was I. Knowing Martin, he'll never have patience to learn the game but obviously we weren't there for that, we were at the bleacher three times a week for other reasons. Martin was blushing when I teased him about Dave Moore, the guy was cute I have to say, and I applauded Martin for his taste. I didn't know that he would take a buffed muscled guy for his type, but we were bffs and whoever he likes, was good enough for me. Every time Dave scores, Martin cheered for him. A normal jock with an ego would hate this but Dave was nice enough to shed Martin a smile and shyly ran his fingers through his short brown hair. This gesture earned him extra points for me.

"He's nice" I said. I was sitting on the bleacher while drinking diet coke.

"I know! He's the best!" Martin exclaimed as he turned around to face me. He'd been standing since the game started. Martin's face was beaming with excitement; he looked like he was in trance with his happiness. The smile was plastered on his face.

"Did you see that? He smiled at me" Martin said, giggling.

"Yes, I saw it. You deserved it though" I told him.

Martin sat beside me; a smile was glued on his face. Then a shadow passed over him and suddenly his expression changed, seemingly musing.

"Are you okay?" I asked.

Martin nodded as he turned to face me. "Do you think Dave... Never mind, are you ready to go?" He didn't finish his first question. I saw anxiousness forming in his eyes, but he immediately brushed it off and stood up, he was facing the field this time. The team was still out there huddling with Coach Monroe. I had no idea what Martin was thinking, I assumed that it was about Dave. I wished I could answer his question or grant his wishes if it's a chance with Dave that he was asking for... I really wanted him to be happy. I felt sad for Martin and I didn't push him with questions as I stood up and pulled up my belongings beside me. I wanted him to know that I'm here for him always. Dave was nice but I think he's straight. I reached and patted Martin's back and we walked together out from the bleacher to the parking lot. The sun already set, and it was nearly dusk. The parking lot was almost empty save for the few cars probably belonging to the athletes and faculties. We reached Martin's car first and we bid each other goodbye. My car was in the back-side area and I had to walk a short distance to reach it. I put on an earphone and blasted my playlist in the background. I wasn't comfortable being alone in a deserted parking lot, so I walked faster this time. Halfway to my car, a huge hand touched my shoulder that made me jump with fear. I tripped and my bag fell on the ground as I released an awful scream.

"Lola it's me! I'm sorry... I didn't mean to..." When I recovered, my eyes were huge to see the person standing in front of me. I knew this guy; he was the captain of the Eagles team. It was Seb, "the Sebastian Whyte", the most famous guy in school.

"Sabastian?" I was astounded.

"I'm sorry Lola; I didn't mean to scare you." His voice was genuinely apologetic. The guy just got out of practice and I could see he hadn't changed his clothes yet. From the looks of it, I hinted that he ran all the way from the field to catch me here because he was still catching his breath and sweating all over. His wavy blonde hair was damped and his light blue eyes lighted up while breathing heavily. He looked so hot that I didn't mind the fact that he hadn't hit the shower yet. Gross I know. Looking like he just got out of a sport magazine photo shoot with his gears dangling on his side. I stared at him waiting for him to say something, forgetting that my stuff was still on the ground. When I realized that it was too late, he already dropped his gears and bent over to get mine. He handed it over to me and I managed to say thanks.

"You scared me there." I said.

"I'm so sorry." His forehead wrinkled with concern.

"It's fine. I'm okay." I stuttered. I looked at him and saw him looking at me. He was so handsome and tall that he was literally dwarfing me. I felt awkward staring at him, so I lowered my gaze and stared on the ground. My toes were pointing each other; it was a signal how awkward the situation was. Finally, he cleared his throat and I looked at him again.

" Uhmmm... I just want to... by the way I'm..." I sensed his nervousness.

"I know who you are..." I said.

"Right... okay... wow..." He smiled then he exhaled heavily trying to distress the nerve he'd been feeling. It was cute, watching Seb making his moves. It took all my strength to hold myself from giggling.

"I'm wondering if you, if you would like to go out with me sometimes?" His voice was soft and hoping and I found it adorable.

"Like a date?" I asked, smiling.

"Yeah?"

Chapter 2

Back at Barry's, the crowd was thickening by the minute and most of them were teenagers trying to get wasted and have fun. I recognized most of them but there were others whom I wasn't familiar with. We snaked into the throng of dancing people headed by Martin. I was trailing behind him trying not to lose his back. Martin knew a lot of them, and his hands were flying every now and then to wave and say Hi. At last, we emerged at the back near the game room; the billiard tables were crowded mostly with boys playing. We were lucky to find a table at the corner near the window overseeing the parking lot. Outside there were still cars coming in, I'm not sure if this was going to lay low any sooner, as the cliché goes: The night's still young. The waiter cleared the table and we sat. I tried to breathe heavily to ease myself, but the fog of cigarette smoke was too strong that made me cough. The entire diner transformed into a bar and it was hysterical.

"You knew a lot of them?" I asked Martin, shouting for him to hear me from the loud music, referring to the crowd.

"I knew some of them by their faces, but I called them darlings, so I don't know their names." He said, shrugging.

I mentally wrote a note to myself immediately, if you don't know their names, used the endearment like Dear, Darling, Sweetheart or Honey or just simply Girl etc. As if I could pull that of... I couldn't imagine calling someone else Sweetheart to say the least. Martin raised a hand gracefully and signaled for a waiter to come.

"We should get a drink!" He said excitedly.

"I'll just have a diet coke" I told him.

He looked at me like I was crazy, and I suddenly braced myself to defend my choice of refreshment. I don't drink alcohol – that's just that. Martin sighed and rolled his eyes and I felt relieved that he didn't make a big deal out of it. The waiter came and moved his ear closer to Martin's mouth to get his order. The waiter left and Martin was staring at his back.

"What?" I asked.

"His cute!" He said smiling.

"Spare him. He's busy, let him do his job." I told him jokingly.

Martin considered this for a while and laughed. His laughter was infectious and so we suddenly burst into laughing.

"Let's dance!" He exclaimed.

"Where?" I immediately panicked. Aside from the fact that there wasn't room to showcase our dance moves, I couldn't dance. I mean, it's not that I couldn't, I didn't know how to... The idea of me dancing scared the shit out of me.

"Here! Come on Lola! As if everyone cares." He insisted. He was already standing up and waiting for me. I looked around and he was right. Nobody would care if I would jump up and down and roll on the floor because everybody was busy wiping the floor with their dancing prowess.

"There's no dance floor" I said, trying to lay my last card.

"Come on! Let's just stand here near the table." He lent a hand and without further protest I took it. There's no use having an argument you couldn't win.

Martin put on his gear and exploded into a sequence of dancing moves. I was dizzy watching him that I almost thought he was doing a mixture of taekwondo and yoga poses. I had no idea what sort of dancing he was doing. Then suddenly he was rapidly juggling his butt that nearly dropped my jaw. I wasn't sure if he was doing African dance with his butt, but I knew he got that from somewhere else. I did my best to follow the rhythm of the music, but my movement was bored and unsure. I swayed my head back and forth and that's all I got.

"What are you doing?" Martin asked while still doing his thing.

"What are YOU doing?" My eyes darted to the butt moves.

"Girl, this is what you called Twerking!" He said proudly amplifying the butt moves.

"What!?!" I was confused.

"Haven't you seen Miley Cyrus' video? This is the Miley move. Here let me teach you." He offered.

I was horrified. Martin pushed me to do twerking several times, but I'd rather be dead. Our orders were already on the table when I looked back, the waiter placed it there without even informing us. Probably he was also appalled to see Martin's twerking moves and just fled the moment he delivered our food. I took a sipped on my diet coke and Martin grabbed his beer. I didn't know Martin ordered a few bunches of food, a plate of hot chili wings which was our favorite then the new burritos and fries. The food looked delicious that I wanted to sit down right away and wolfed over it but Martin wasn't done twerking yet. I stood right there with my diet coke in hand trying to figure out my moves. I looked around and the place was literally foggy with cigarette smoke. People were jumping up and down, some were twirling their hips while others were awkwardly doing running man moves and it was ridiculous. The roof was going down, and everybody was shouting and having a great time. From all the chaos inside the diner, a figure appeared in the corner that nearly took my breath away. Suddenly, I became conscious of my movement that I soon realized that I was no longer dancing. I was standing there staring at the figure in front of me. With lips slightly parted, intense blue eyes staring straight at me, blond wavy hair neatly comb – he looked so right that everybody in the diner looked so wrong including me. Seb smiled as he walked slowly towards me. I was wearing a simple white blouse and a pair of skinny jeans- I started doubting my style of clothing now that Seb was here. He was gorgeous. Just a plain shirt, brown khaki pants and a pair of snickers and he was perfect. No extra effort.

When he reached me, he smiled showing his perfect dents. Dimples appeared both of his cheeks, he looked ravishing. My knees started to weaken and the urge to fidget was inevitable. That didn't look good for a girl to stand fidgeting in front of a boy, so I stood my ground and inhaled to calm my nerves.

"Hi there!" Seb greeted me. He was near enough that I smelled Dove scented soap from his skin. It was a pleasant smell and he wasn't wearing any perfume.

"Hi" I said shyly.

Then we were quiet for a while, awkwardly staring at each other waiting for someone to break the spell first. Then we heard a gasp that made Seb and I turned to where the overstated sound came from. The sight of the fabulous Frey in shock was the best thing ever like he saw an apparition appeared in front of him. Jaw dropped, hands on his face, huge eyes like it were about to pop out of its socket. The twerking was over and all he did was stand in front of us gawking at Sebastian who was amused as I was. He probably didn't notice Seb approaching earlier and to see the captain of the Eagles team with me caught him off guard. Martin darted his eyes from Seb to mine and vise-versa. I could sense that he was still recovering from his shock and trying to absorb what was happening.

My face turned to see Sebastian trying to hold a laugh and the effect was spontaneous and this made me want to join him. But I gripped myself so I could introduce the two of them.

"Martin, this is Sebastian Whyte." I said. Martin already found his mouth on the floor and closed it.

"Sebastian this is my best friend... Martin Frey" Seb extended a hand to shake Martin's, whom with his eagerness to hold Seb's hand took it right away and covered it with his other hand like he was reading Seb's future.

"It's an honor to meet you Sebastian..." said Martin.

"You can call me Seb... the pleasure is mine." Seb said politely.

"Seb... I mean..." Martin was still holding Seb's hand and with no intention of letting it go. I rolled my eyes and told them to stop with the formality. I realized that if I didn't do this, Martin would start bowing and call Seb his highness. We moved to the table and sat. Seb sat beside me while Martin was on the other side facing us. The two of them bonded instantly like they've known each other for so long as they talked about their trips during the summer. My head was turning left and right like a Ping-Pong ball listening to their crazy adventures. Seb went to Thailand then Cambodia to see the temples and then they went to Boracay Island in the Philippines. He said the Island was a paradise and the beaches were picture perfect. He and his family had a blast. Martin's eyes lit up when he heard about the beaches and told Seb about his escapades in Brazil that he stayed in a Cabana while sipping mojitos. I was sort of left out with the discussion because I was the only one who stayed in Silent Hills the entire summer. So, I just sat quietly and listened. Seb was cool with Martin, he was really a nice guy or probably because he knew that Martin was my best friend. That didn't matter. If he treated Martin fairly then he earned my trust. I couldn't stand boys having prejudice against gay people. Seriously, homophobes are getting old. They're here to stay, besides, girls like me needs our gay best friend.

Someone might be asking if I knew Seb before. The answer was yes, I knew him. He was the most popular guy in school, even people from the Facility Department knew him. Young girls working in the cafeteria held their breath when he was around. But I was the girl who was satisfied with my anonymity. I normally turned the other way and hid in my own little corner, away from the spotlight. I never got the chance to come close to Seb; mostly he was at the field practicing or in the cafeteria and in the hallway with his teammates. He was surrounded by lots of people and the thought of pushing it was even a pathetic idea. I never aspired to have someone who was too high to reach so I never thought of even knowing him personally. He was sort of an enigma for me like Brad Pitt was an enigma.

Then there was Jessa King, shoulder length hair, bangs, green eyes, pouty lips, beautiful legs; rich parents – you get the idea: the perfect dream girl. She was the embodiment of what girls in school aspired to become. Well, aside from the fact that she was mean and rude to people who didn't belong to her clique – that didn't make her desirable in my list. But who cares about my list anyway...? Everybody expected Seb to be with Jessa. I mean the two of them made sense – the most gorgeous guy with the most popular girl equals perfect couple alert. When gossip started circling around campus about Seb and me, my twitter feeds flooded with foul accusations calling me slut, wannabe, whore, strong words telling me that I wasn't good enough for Seb; I decided to quit social media and deleted my account. But it was almost at the end of the school year and that was a whole week of humiliation before summer break. When I passed by Jessa and her minions along the hallway before the school ended, I could almost feel their eyes glaring and clawing at my back, but I bowed my head and ignored them. The gossip circulated and it didn't last long because everybody was excited planning for their summer vacation. I took that as an advantage. The chance I got with Martin was minimal, we were cramming for finals and I didn't want to be selfish to talk about my own predicament when both of us had exams to think about. After the parking lot incident, Seb was regularly texting me asking how I was. He kept apologizing for everything because he probably knew how mean those accusations were. To compensate, a bunch of surprises awaited me in my car every afternoon. Flowers given to me by the Eagles team, balloons and chocolates etc., anything that he could think of to make me feel better. The effort was well appreciated; after all I'm still a girl. When we were at the parking lot, I told Seb that he'd get his answer if I would go out on a date with him after finals. So, I wasn't surprised when my Mom knocked on my door after I got home from school on a Friday telling me I had a visitor. At first, I thought it was Martin, but he was a regular visitor in our house that my mom was used to him coming in and out. For the record Martin would just normally bolt in my room and ransacked my closet. This time it was different, my mom was giving me an accusatory look.

"Who is it?" I asked.

"It's a boy." She said, with brows arched and eyes suddenly teasing.

"He's a friend." I said defensively.

"I'm not saying anything." She said giving me a wink before she disappeared from the door.

I stared at myself in the mirror. My tangled hair needed combing, there were dark shades around my eyes probably from the late night of studying. I had few freckles in my gaunt face; my light green eyes were staring back at me. I looked down to my drawer and grabbed a comb.

Seb was waiting for me outside our house, leaning over the side of his black convertible BMW. He stood up when he saw me coming. He was smiling as I approached, I smiled back. My heart leaped as the space between us closed. There was something about Seb's presence that made me nervous and excited at the same time. He made me gasp and knocked the air out of me. When I looked at him, suddenly the world stopped turning and all I could see was him, like he was the only one breathing, tangible and alive. My emotion was getting ahead of me; I made a mental note not to rely on it when I'm around Seb. I couldn't afford a betrayal by my own sentiments toward him, not when I had no idea what I truly felt. After the Parking lot incident, he entered my mind and took over. I could daydream about him the whole day and set aside finals. Checking my phone every five minutes became a habit during the final week. I couldn't get enough of Seb. Every time I see him at the parking lot waiting for me, I always have the urge to run towards him and lock him in a tight embrace. The way he talked to me and looked at me, like I was the only one in the world that mattered to him. His voice calling my name was music to my ears, his scent intoxicated me, when I stared deep into his eyes – I saw the entire sky kingdom trapped within it – bright blue eyes beaming expressively.

"Hey..." I greeted first. He made one step forward; both hands were on his back pocket. Seb didn't say a word; his smile turned into a grin that made him look more irresistible. His eyes were questioning, doing all the talking. I knew that he was waiting for my answer, but I wanted him to say something, to ask me once again.

"What?" I said absent mindedly.

"So... Final is over..." He said.

"Yeah... Finally, ... Can't wait for summer." I said nonchalantly.

I couldn't stare at his eyes any longer; the fear that I would not be able to restrain myself and threw my arms around him put me in check. I let my eyes drift looking for distraction, anything that could break me from his spell.

"Uhm... About my..."

"It's already late." I said cutting him trying to look at my watch. "Is tomorrow okay?" My cheeks suddenly felt warm. I looked down to hide my blush. When I didn't receive a response from Seb, I panicked. I looked up and caught him staring at me. His mouth was opened in between laughter and shock. He was overjoyed. A big smile broke in his face that made his dimples appear. Agitated suddenly that he didn't know what to do like a kid in Disneyland.

"Wow... Do you really want to go out with me?" He asked reassuringly. "Is that a yes?"

"Yes." I said shyly.

Then we were distracted by someone. Seb and I turned to see who it was, it was Ram. My brother arrived from who-knows-where. He stopped and stared at us scornfully then went his way... I faced Seb and wanted to apologize but he chuckled as if telling me that he understood.

"Okay, Uhmmm... tomorrow then..." He pursed his lips as if thinking and slowly turned around to go.

I stared at his back as he walked to his car. Before he hopped in, he glanced at me and winked. This gesture made me laugh. I waved him goodbye as he got inside the car. It was already dark when the taillight of his BMW disappeared from the corner of River Gate Avenue. I turned around and went back inside the house to find my mom preparing for dinner. Ram went straight to his room as usual. She looked up as I walked to the dining room lamely. My mother gave me a knowing look as she watched me move closer. She stopped what she was doing and welcomed me with a hug. This was great about our mom; she always knew when we needed a mother's touch or her approval on anything. We didn't have to ask her or tell her that we needed a hug – she was there at our side, ready to take our pain. I missed her; I should have spent time with her when I got the chance. We could have the entire day doing girly stuff. But I already passed my chances of doing all of that and what I've got was merely wishful thinking as I stared at the burning skyline outside my window. It was always like that here in the Fourth Realm, known as the lowest part of the spirit world. The weather was always humid in the daytime, but the temperature dropped dramatically at night. The infernal sky burned red as if painted in a canvas. But we'll get to the limbo later or what the living famously known as The Purgatory.

Seb was already in our living room talking to my mom at 3PM the next day when I got down from my room. He told me to wear something casual and comfortable. I wasn't sure how casual he wanted me to be, so I settled on a blue T and a pair of jeans. When he looked up, his eyes sparkled like water in the ocean. He stood up and waited for me to come down. I saw two cups of tea on the table and I had a feeling that Seb and my mom had a blast chatting. From the looks of it, my mom was all smiles as I caught her eyes. Seb won her over it was obvious. Seb told my mother that he would take me home early and my mom gave us her blessing right away. Just like that...

"What did you do to my mom?" I teased him in the car.

"I didn't do anything. We were just talking." He said smiling.

"What did you talk about?"

"The usual..."

The car ran smoothly on the highway. Inside I didn't notice how fast it was, but I didn't seem to care. I wasn't looking at the view outside anyway; I was more distracted with the sight of Seb sitting next to me. He drove the vehicle with ease that it was sort of meditational – as if the car was an extension of him. Not to mention how sensational he looked in the driver seat. I couldn't stop glancing.

"Where are we going?" I asked. I noticed we were already leaving town.

"It's a surprise." He said, glancing at my side and winked. What's up with the winking part?

We were miles away from town and the car went on going deeper to the south. We passed through open fields, copses and swampy areas. Probably 30 minutes of driving, finally the car slowed and turned right from the highway. Seb opened the windows and the fresh air and smells of water hinted to me that there was a swamp up ahead. I was right with water; the car halted in an open restaurant, at the back overlooking the Mississippi river. Seb told me that this was the place for people looking for sweet escape. The view at the back was spectacular; we chose a table at the corner near the railing. I stood there with my hands on the railing steel gazing at the magnificent river, far ahead the sun starting to climb down painting the sky red.

"Wow" Was the only thing I could utter.

"It wasn't called Magic Restaurant for nothing." Seb said.

Who the hell named their restaurant Magic? Certainly, there's one. When I turned to face him, Seb was gazing at the river. The shade of the sun fading from afar giving him a certain glow. He looked down and caught me staring at him. Immediately I retracted and turned around embarrassed. He reached for my chin and made me face him. When I opened my eyes once again, I was held captive by the magnet of his stares. His eyes captured me passionately that it was even impossible to resist.

"You are so beautiful Lola." He whispered.

He leaned closer towards me and my heart thudded beneath my ribcage. My body shivered inside by his touch and I was alienated by it. I've never been touched by a guy before, not like this. Not the way Seb touched my face. Martin was an exception to the rules of course. His face was inches away from me, we were that close that I was drunk by the brilliant sapphire color of his eyes. His breath was fresh and smelled like menthol, lips slightly opened and inviting. If I couldn't break this moment, I was afraid that I wouldn't be able to stop what was inevitable to happen. But I didn't want it to stop, I wanted to kiss him. I wanted to taste the softness of his kiss and melt in the warmth of his embrace. But it was too early for that... I gathered all my strength and reached deeper inside of me to find my own freewill. I needed to break free. When my own strength was more than enough to detoxify my mind, I inhaled deeply and smiled.

"Carrot Cake" I said the first thing that came to my head.

"What?" He asked, astonished.

"I mean, do they serve Carrot Cake here?" My head turned to look around as if searching for the waiter to take our order.

"I think so... They have the best Strawberry shake." He said smiling. The spell was broken, and I felt relieved. I was so close to giving myself all over to him, but I prevented it. I was proud of my will power.

Chapter 3

The Sunset view from Magic Restaurant lingered in my mind. It was captivating. Though I wondered if it feels the same if I went there alone without Seb. For the record, I was with Seb when I stood there gazing at the Mississippi river and it was indeed our first date before he went away for summer vacation. It was our little haven, a place where we spend time without interruption. I knew it was stupid, but I didn't want to admit that I missed him. I didn't want to entertain the possibility that I might have feelings for him. I was afraid to admit that every day I woke up excited knowing that the faster the day passed; the closer I get to his return. He promised to send me postcard to every destination they visited with his family and he was true to that promise. I reminisced about the time we spent sipping strawberry shake and eating carrot cake at Magic as I listened back and forth to Seb and Martin talking. They had surely found their common ground and I was happy about it while I retreated to my own corner in my mind. Seb glanced at me occasionally checking if I was okay. I smiled encouragingly at him. I wanted him to know that it's important for me for him and Martin to get along. I could wait. Besides, watching him interacted with Martin was a treat enough. The diner was already full of woozy people and because most of them were puffing cigarettes, the absence of breathable air suffocated me. I decided that it was time to go. My watch told me that I was an hour late for dinner and when I checked my phone, there were 4 missed calls from my mom.

"Shit!" I chortled. Seb and Martin looked at me at the same time.

"What is it? Are you okay?" Seb asked while I was still staring at my iPhone. I looked up at him and simpered.

"I'm fine but... I told my mom that I will be home before dinner." I said.

"I'm one hour late." I gave him a sorry look.

"Relax Lola; we're having a great time. Besides, it's not like you're doing illegal or something." Martin said.

"It's my mom." I blurted.

Seb stood up immediately and offered to take me home. I was surprised by this but my heart flipped with joy knowing that I would have him alone on our way home to River Gate even for a short time. I went out from the booth and gave Martin a hug. I told him that I would be fine, and I couldn't wait for our first day as junior high students. Martin giggled with me as he returned my embrace. When we were done, Martin went to address Seb, giving him mean girl look while telling him to be nice to me. I smiled with the idea that my best friend was serious on keeping me safe. The picture of Martin throwing cashmere camisole and designer clutch bag at Seb entered my mind and it took all of my force to hold myself from laughing.

"Yes sir. I'll take good care of her." Seb vowed jokingly.

"Okay. Get out of here. I have some serious dancing to do... and that waiter is sooo..." Martin was already walking away from us and I didn't get his last word. He disappeared into the crowd. Seb and I looked at each other and giggled. He guided me as we moved into the multitude of sweating bodies looking for the exit. He never left my side until we reached the door. The diner was so full that other customers took their drink outside. The music pulsated in the beat of RnB songs and people were busy talking in clusters. We were on our way to the parking lot when we heard a male voice calling Seb. Both of us turned around and found Dave Moore running towards us. He was wearing a polo shirt, cargo shorts and snickers. I imagined Martin drooling over him when he saw him like this. This Dave guy was cute as hell despite of his buff physique.

"Hey Whyte! Wait up" He said.

The two of them broke into a silly male handshake moves. I didn't get why boys have to do that or probably it wasn't meant for me to understand it. I wondered if boys felt the same thing toward girls when we kiss on the cheek as way of greeting each other. When they were done, Seb introduced me to Dave who extended his huge hand to shake mine.

"So... you're the famous Lola that the Eagles were talking about huh?" He said teasing. I gnawed and darted my eyes to see Seb trying to hide his red face. He was blushing and my heart was rolling with flattery to see this. I took Dave's hand and shook it. I looked at his face to see what Martin saw in him. He was cute, that was given, adorable to say the least. I noticed his eyes sparkled in the dim light, was that hazel brown? His smile radiates a happy disposition. This was the guy who could brighten up a room and I'm not even kidding. He made me feel happy while just talking to him.

"I guess that's me." I told him. I looked at Seb who was currently observing us. He was pursing his lips, arms curled in front of his chest. His face came back to its normal color. I looked down to see how small my hand compared to Dave's.

"Okay that's enough; let her go." Seb said flippantly.

"Oh right, sorry." Dave chuckled. He gave my hand a little squeeze and released.

"So, are you two are together now?" Seb and I stiffened with how forthright Dave question was. He shot arrows we didn't know where it came from. I raised my eyebrows as I faced Seb who looked stunned as I was. Probably Dave realized how awkward we were, and side stepped embarrassed by his question, realizing his mistake.

"I'm sorry man, I didn't mean to..." It was his time to turn red. He looked at Seb apologetically then at me. I felt sorry for him, his baby face sunk like a boy deprived with his toy gun.

Seb tapped Dave on the shoulder and told him it was okay. When his eyes flashed ruefully on me, my heart melted to see how remorseful he was... I wanted to reach out for him and hug him but instead a lenient smile was enough to let him know that I wasn't offended, probably offhanded but no harmed done.

Dave sprinted back to the diner, his broad shoulders heaving as he went away. I turned around and started walking to the parking lot, Seb walked beside me. We didn't speak for a while, walking in silence under the canopy of the only florescent light illuminating the area. The air was warm and dry, the sky gleamed with the myriad starlight, but it was a moonless night. The dead air stretched between us until Seb cleared his throat and spoke.

"So... How's your summer?" He asked.

"It was fine. Nothing fancy I guess." I chuckled. I didn't want to elaborate how I'd spent my day thinking about him. "Thanks for the postcards by the way." I added.

"Yeah? Did you receive all of it?" He asked. I looked at him and saw the outline of his lips forming a smile.

"All of it." I said.

We halted in front of his car. I stared at the BMW like I've never seen it before. The midnight color of the car shone as if greeting me.

"I missed him too..." Seb said wryly.

"Yeah... Me too." I said.

He opened the front-seat door and escorted me in. Closing it carefully after I got in, he sprinted around and took the driver seat. Again, the feeling of fascination took over me, the way I was captivated by the sight of Seb driving. He reminded me of that old movie Knight Rider with David Hasselhoff that my dad loved so much. I know it's far-off, but I couldn't help it. Seb started the engine and the car came to life right away. We got out of the parking lot, leaving the sight of the diner with people crammed outside trying to get in. In a matter of minute, we were driving around town heading for the highway. We passed through the piazza in front of the post office to see the night bazaar. There were several booths selling different colorful items and people were crowding around looking for something to buy. For a moment I wanted to tell Seb to park the car somewhere so we could check but time was ticking, and mom was going to kill me if I'd stay longer. Seb was amazed as I was to see the town filled with people, locals were out in the street walking in shorts and flip-flops with their families. On the other side the cafes and restaurants were full, customers were dining in fancy clothes and some were just simply hanging out with friends sipping refreshments. My mind went through the dates in the calendar thinking if there's a town celebration I missed.

"Is this normal?" I finally asked Seb. I was intrigued by the sudden event going on outside.

"I don't know. Did we miss something?" His eyes fizzed excitedly.

When I met his eyes, I shrugged. "It's probably nothing. Maybe it's the last weekend before school starts on Monday" I said and faced the front view of the car to avoid his gaze. In my peripheral vision, I saw Seb nodded in agreement to what I said.

"Maybe" He said.

Because of the volume of people out in the street, Seb drove the car slowly and stopped intermittently to let people passed. My eyes wandered outside enjoying the festivity. But before we reached the corner and hit the main highway, I noticed a black CRV parked on the side of the road in front of an open bar with a neon green sign that said Olive Bar. The car looked familiar, I thought. I was denying what I already knew; it was my father's car. I wondered what he was doing there; he was probably with his comrade. I reasoned that my dad was busy at work; he might be there in his place right now preparing for sleep, he didn't have time for leisure like this. I realized how selfish I was the moment I think that, and I was embarrassed of myself. Besides, what do I know? My father lived alone, and I had no idea what his days like. When he visited us during weekends, we normally talked about schools and our interests or anything to update him about what was going on in our lives. Sometimes he took Ram and me to go out biking on the park, on rainy days our living room transformed into a fraternity den with him and Ram beating each other with video games. It was all about us, we never really talked about him.

I asked Seb to drive slowly and went on explaining that I thought I saw my father's car. He asked me where it was, and I pointed on the black CRV on the other side of the street. His eyes followed my finger and I saw him looked up to see the sign. He smiled wryly and turned to face me.

"Your dad knows how to choose a place to hang out." He said.

"What do you mean?" I was confused. I suddenly felt worried about my dad. My current apprehension was probably written all over my face that Seb immediately reached out to touch my hand. I was startled by this and I marveled on how my body reacted with his touch. His hand was warmed against mine. I was distracted and I almost forgot about my dad, but I was determined to know what he was doing at the bar.

Yes, he was probably chilling out with his friends or... I immediately cleared my head, I didn't want to entertain the thought of my dad with someone else other than my mom but as I have said, I was embarrassed with my selfishness. Seb made a U turn on the other side of the road, he didn't say a thing about the bar, but his support was well appreciated. It's not that I wanted to spy on my dad, what he did with his friends during wee hours was none of my business but my urged to know more about him was too strong. As a daughter I wanted to take the responsibility of knowing our parents - I wanted to know the person rather than calling them Mom and Dad. Seb parked the BMW few feet away from my father's car; he turned off the light and the engine.

"It was probably nothing. This is an open bar so... There's nothing you have to worry about." Seb said. I looked at him and felt that there was something he wasn't telling me. I could feel his anxious about it, but he was also worried that the information would upset me.

"Seb, what is it? What is this place?" I asked him. "I know there is something you wanted to tell me. Come on spiel. I can handle it, I promise." I challenged.

Seb looked straight to my eyes and he waited for me to back out but I clenched my teeth and held my gaze. When he realized that I was serious, he sighed heavily and dropped the stares, slouched back to the car seat, eyes straight in front recollecting.

"Every time my parents had a huge fight, it always ends up the same. My dad left the house after to cool down. Sometimes he came home before dawn and slept at the guest room, often he returned the next day. When my mom asked him where he slept, the alibi was, he checked-in in a hotel." He paused.

"You don't believe him?" I asked.

"No. I'm not buying it." Seb shook his head.

"One time I followed him." His eyes flashed towards the Olive Bar sign.

"And you found him here?" I asked softly, my eyes drifted towards the bar. Seb nodded to answer my question. It wasn't pleasant I could tell; retelling it didn't just bring back bad memories but painful feelings as well. I didn't ask him to tell me everything, but I wanted him to know that I was here for him if that was the least thing that I could do.

"I followed him to the bar. I didn't want him to know that I was there because I knew that he wouldn't like that. It was a bar for adult but...well technically I'm not legal yet. But it was an open bar... I just wanted to make sure that he was okay." Seb paused, his eyes wandered outside.

"He was with someone else. A guy, early thirties, brunette, tall..." He said.

"Probably a co-worker, drinking buddies, a friend..." I said considering...

"I know what I saw Lola." Seb faced me then looked away. His face was stern and there was anger in his voice. I saw a different side of Seb that I didn't know before. I wanted to say something, but I decided it would be wise not to... and let his anger subsided.

"I'm sorry, I didn't mean to..." He said apologizing.

I looked at him sympathetically and reached for his arm and gave it a little squeeze. I felt sorry for Seb, I mean, what would I feel if I found out that my father was cheating... with a guy? It wouldn't be a problem if my father is gay, I would be shock of course but he's my father and I would accept him whatever his preferences were... But the cheating part is something that is non-negotiable.

As I was pondering Seb's predicament with his father, two figures appeared from the bar. A female wearing a tiny skirt and a pair of high heels was giggling and laughing. She was accompanied by a man in denim pants and checkered buttoned-down shirt. My eyes almost popped out when I realized that it was my dad. The two of them looked happy - very happy, creepily whispering to each other as they swayed towards the car. Dad's arm was wrapped around the woman's shoulders while hers was draped around my dad's waist. Obviously, they were drinking and my dad looked drunk considering the way he moved as he ushered the woman to his car. I noticed that she was also holding a bottle in her hand and she was waving it left and right as they danced like drunkards normally do. This side of my father was stranger to me and never in my life would have thought that I would see him in this state of intoxication. This person was far away from the loving father that I've known all my life. A part of me wanted to run after him and call his attention, wanted him to know that I was there. I was grateful that Seb was there to pull me back from my senses. I was afraid that I would do things I would regret later. Dad didn't want me to see him like this. I didn't have any business being out here in the first place. This was his private life. He was my dad, but he was a human being who needed his personal space... so was my mom. I needed to get out of here.

I turned to face Seb; my voice failed me as I was trying to swallow tears down my throat. I was relieved that without saying a word, Seb understood the unspoken dispute of my heart by the anguish look in my face. Seb's car roared to life and immediately we took off. The car swerved through the asphalt and in a moment, we were already trailing the highway down to River Gate. I blinked back the tears in my eyes and inhaled deeply to ease myself. It all made sense to me now, the Olive Bar was the place where lonely adult goes to entertain themselves. It's not necessarily a place for hook ups but... I shook my head to clear my mind; I didn't want to judge people. I didn't want to deluge my brain with thoughts that would stain my dad's name. He was still my father after all. He was no longer married to my mom, technically he was single, and he could do whatever he wanted. The drive all the way to the River Gate was swift and Seb and I sat in awkward silence until the car stopped in our driveway. Outside, the front porch light of our house was still on, that only meant one thing - mom was waiting for me to come home.

"Are you okay?" Seb whispered. I was relieved to finally hear him say something. I looked at him and nodded nonchalantly.

"Thank you... for... everything." I said.

His eyes turned darker like the deep ends of the ocean, lips forming a thin line. He gave me a quick nod to tell me that it's nothing.

"I'm sorry about your dad." He paused and reached for my hand. "If you wanted to talk about anything..."

His touch was warm and comforting. The way his skin brushed against mine was reassuring, making me believed that everything would turn out fine. I just wanted to stay this way for a while, but it was getting late and the longer I stayed out, the harder I was in trouble with mom. I pulled my hand from his grasp and placed it on my lap.

"I'd better go... Thank you for taking me home once again..." I managed to give him a sly smile.

He grinned and gave me a sympathetic face. He was very understanding and from that particular moment, I wanted to throw my arms around him, but I held myself and instead reached for the door and went out.

Mom was already waiting in the dining room when I got in. Her hands were on the table capping a mug of hot tea. She looked up to see me walking towards the table. Her face was serious, but she wasn't angry. All she wanted was an explanation. I wasn't good at lying so I decided to just tell her the truth. When I was done talking, she reached out for my hand and squeezed it.

"Do you want me to make you a cup of tea?" She asked beaming.

I nodded excitedly. Who was I to say no with this treat from my mom? All of a sudden, I was a little girl waiting for her to give me my milk. I decided not to tell her anything about my dad as I didn't want to ruin this moment. If she was angry when I came in a while ago, I would have understood - she was worried with my safety. The odd feeling, I felt seeing my dad with someone else was long gone. I felt better now. Who would have thought that a nice conversation with my mom over a cup of tea would make a huge difference? Not knowing that it would be my last conversation with her. The night ended well and that's all that matters. I would repeat those memories in my head time and time again, for the rest of eternity.

When I came down the next day, I found my mom in the kitchen making pancakes. I offered to help but she shunned me, telling that she got it covered. I didn't like the feeling of being useless, but I couldn't help it if my mom didn't want me in the kitchen. Instead of standing there in my pajamas, I went straight to the refrigerator and poured myself a glass of orange juice then went to the living room to scan the channel on the television. I wondered where my brother was, he was probably still in his room asleep. Part of me wanted to talk to him about dad but I was worried about my brother's reaction. Ram worshiped dad so much that I was afraid how hard he would take the idea of our father dating someone else other than our mom. My instinct told me that my brother deserved to know the truth. He would be angry for sure, but I wanted him to hear it from me than someone else.

I turned the television off and sprinted toward the stairs. My mother was still in the kitchen preparing for breakfast and I wanted this conversation to be quick so I could get it out of my system. I knocked on my brother's door and called his name. I heard a groaned and I took it as a sign that he was already awake. Quietly I opened the door and saw him still in bed rubbing his eyes.

"Good morning monster!" I greeted him with a smile.

He looked at me trying to focus. There's a faint dark circle in his eyes probably from sleeping late because of playing video games. He was crazy about it. He would rather play video games the whole day than go to school.

"Lola." He sat up. "What's up?"

I tiptoed to the bed and sat on the corner. I had no idea how I would tell him about dad and I mumbled words as I practiced in my mind. I almost forgot that I was already inside Ram's room and he was staring at me like I was a crazy person.

"Are you talking to yourself?" I could smell sarcasm in his words. This was great; he was in good mood and I was afraid that I was going to ruin it. When I met Ram's eyes he was beaming with a look of victory in his face. He caught me in mere insanity situation talking to myself, he was enjoying this. I could feel my cheeks burned with embarrassment, this was my brother and knowing him, he would use this moment to get even until who-knows-when. I rolled my eyes and sighed, yielding to the fate of his triumph. When I faced him the second time, I was serious.

"I need to tell you something." I said.

"Okay." With a smile coiling his lips. He was teasing me.

"What?"

"Nothing!" His hands were up surrendering and grinning. I knew that he was teasing me with something. "I saw you getting out of Mr. Whyte's car last night."

"Were you spying on me?" My face flushed red that I just wanted to run to my room.

"Well not really, Dad wanted me to look after you, that's all. He said; you will likely to have boyfriend at your age. I'm just following orders you know..." He said.

"What are you, my bodyguard?" I said gawking, he shrugged.

"He is a friend. That's all." I told him, trying to sound normal.

"Alright, I'm just saying."

"Look, I didn't come here for that okay. It's about dad." Words rolled out in my mouth effortlessly. I looked straight into my brother's eyes and wait for a few second.

"What about him?" He asked. The mocking face was all gone now. All of a sudden, he was serious. I didn't know how to say it but I had to believe that it was the best thing to do.

"I saw him with someone else last night at Olive Bar." I said.

"Hoooaaahhh... Did you go to that place? You're so in trouble Lola. If Dad finds out..."

"Wait! I didn't go to that place. I mean I was... I was with Seb and... and we were in his car then I saw dad came out from Olive with a woman." I explained it in one breathing.

"What!?" The confusion was evident in his eyes.

"That's what I am trying to tell you. It's probably nothing. I mean dad is a guy and... She's probably a friend or... I don't know Ram; I don't know what to think. Should I tell mom?" I gave him a worried look.

"No!" Ram almost yelled. "No..." He said it again in a whisper. His eyes were wild looking straight to mine - confirming if I was telling the truth. Of course, I was. Why would I lie facts about my father? Not this, not to my brother.

"Tell me what you actually saw." He said. His brows furrowed as he stared at me waiting. I swallowed and I started from the beginning. I told him about what the woman looked like, how her arm snaked around our father's waist. I told him everything what he needed to know. When I was done Ram was staring at me blankly. I whispered his name and asked him what he was thinking. He might be my younger brother, but I couldn't underestimate his way of thinking. For some aspect he was immature but, in this situation, he had more sense than I was.

"We cannot tell mom about it, Lola. I know they'd been separated for long now but... well, eventually if dad is serious about this woman and he wanted to marry her... he will have the decency to introduce her to us. Besides, we're his family too..." He paused and waited for me to absorb what he just said.

"What do we do?" I asked feeling helpless.

"We don't have to do anything. Look, it's their personal life." He said referring to our parents and reached for my shoulder. "I'm sorry that you had to see that alone. I wish I was there with you."

"Thank you, Ram. At least I can get this out of my system now that you know." I gave him a sympathetic look. "Will you be okay?"

"I'll be fine. He's still our dad no matter what." He said smirking.

"Yes, and you're still my baby brother... So, get up now. Mom made pancakes for breakfast." I was on my way to the door.

"Hey Lola..." He called. I glanced back at him.

"It'll be our secret right?"

"Our little secret." I said before I closed the door of his room.

Chapter 4

It was probably four months ago when it happened or so I thought. The thing about the spirit world, time didn't run the way it used to in the world of the living. An hour here was probably a week in Idmuria, meaning Earth, the living world - that's what they called it. When darkness engulfed me after the crash, I remember feeling very cold. As if blanketed in velvet snow, I shivered furiously as I coiled into fetal position. The freezing didn't stay long, when it passed, I was embraced in warm sensation, easing my body and calming my veins. When I opened my eyes, I realized that I was lying on the ground. Slowly I sat up and looked around me. I was alone on the side of the road. The memory of the accident flashed before me, I saw the rear front of the truck hitting Rose, crushing me along with it. Rose, my compact red swift Suzuki was pressed beyond recognition. The flashback made me shiver. I stood up and looked for bruises but there was nothing. I was perfectly fine. I held both of my arms as I walked towards the center of the road. Rose was nowhere to be found and so was the truck. I wondered where the truck driver was. There was nothing in here, I was totally alone.

I turned around again to see the narrowed street; it was endless. This couldn't be the Highway in Silent Hills. I remember the accident took place in a crossroad but there was no intersection here. There were untamed copses on each side, giving me an eerie vibe, this street was abandoned.

"Where am I?" I whispered mostly to myself.

"You're in Purgatory." A female voice shattered the silence. I turned around to see who it was. I winced and took one step back when I saw her. A girl, probably a few years older than me was standing a few feet away. Cladding in black leather tight pants and jacket, she looked severely geared up. On her right hand she was holding a weapon that looked like a samurai sword, long and gleaming. On the other hand, she was holding a gun, it looked like a gun, but it was bigger and longer. Her emerald eyes were perusing me curiously. Red lips mirroring the fiery hair that was loosely tied. Her skin was milk white giving her a brutal look, yet beautiful. Badass as she seemed, I stared at her with amazement. My hands covering my awed struck face while my eyes were huge in shock. She must saw how stupefied I was and realized that I wasn't a threat. Her body relaxed a bit and put the gun out; slides back the sword in its scabbard and slung it on her back. She walked towards me; her movement was serene and graceful. I tensed as I watched her approached but I didn't make a move. I stood my ground and held my gaze. I saw her confidence as she moved as if she was ready for anything. When she was a foot away from me, her eyes steadied as she spoke.

"I'm sorry about your death. I'm Olga." She extended her hand.

My hand was shaking when I reached for hers but her gripped was strong and warm. My mind clung to what she said about being sorry for my death. Am I dead? I thought.

"I'm Lola." I said; my voice was breaking.

"Nice to meet you Lola. Tell you what, I'm glad to give you a warm welcome but we need to get off the road right away. It's not safe." She said calmly.

"Where am I? What am I doing here?" I asked feeling confused.

"I'll explain it to you later. Right now, we need to move." She looked anxious, head glancing from left to right.

"Come with me and try not to make a noise if you can." She turned around ready to go and I followed in acquiesce. I wasn't familiar of this place and if there was danger up ahead as she stated, I'd rather stuck beside Lara Croft here with her sword than somewhere else. Right, her name was Olga, but she reminded me of that movie Tomb Raider. We walked silently and I was trying very hard to follow her pace. We got off the road and entered the groves. Walking behind Olga made me saw how alert she was yet careful not to make unnecessary noise. I on other hand was carrying all the noises unfortunately. Well, you couldn't blame me; try walking in doll shoes on the forest. My feet were making crisp noises as I stepped on dried foliage; the ground was covered with it. For an instance Olga stopped. Her hand signaling me to stop moving and so I did. While I stood there waiting for Olga's instruction, I realized that all my senses were heightened. I could feel the changes in the air, I could hear noises from the variety of animals in the forest then there was something else that I couldn't pin point. My eyes darted towards Olga; she was already angling to face me. I wanted to ask her what it was but then she signaled a finger on her mouth telling me not to make a sound. I bit my lips immediately. Then the air changed, I smelled gas all around as the surrounding atmosphere became constraint that I was suddenly having a hard time breathing. I brought a hand to cover my nose. Olga tiptoed slowly to my side and her face moved closer to my ear.

"Hold your breath." She whispered.

But before I could make a response, a dark smoke appeared in front of us snaking behind the trees. I heard Olga cursed as she pushed me to the ground. I fell, face down but I retorted immediately to face her.

"Take cover. When you see the smokes coming after you, run. They found us." She said, her emerald eyes beaming with both excitement and fear.

"Who are they?" I asked scared.

"Darklings... Now move!"

Olga didn't bother to explain. Her eyes shifted to the front, fierce and ready. A smile broke in her face as she moved forward crawling like a panther. She left me scrambling and exposed. I didn't wait for anyone to see me. My instinct told me that if I'm not going to move immediately, I would be an easy target. I didn't want to be a sitting duck waiting to be discovered. I wondered what they would do if they caught me; it's not that they could kill me, I'm already dead. Well, that's what Olga said. Still, that didn't make any sense; you cannot kill someone else twice. I could hear voices and among those voices were Olga's. I covered my ears when I heard gun firing followed by growls.

Those weren't human growls, I thought. Then I remember what Olga told me a while ago, Darklings, those growling were probably from them. I wasn't sure, I haven't seen one yet. Then I heard metal colliding. I heard Olga screamed and I was startled by it. I wanted to look but I was afraid that the Darklings might see me. Besides, the fog descended on the ground and the groves was covered with smokes all around. I still saw dark smokes moving swiftly behind trees and I ducked back on the ground and covered my head. I couldn't see what was happening and to push it would be ridiculous. I rest my case and decided to stay hidden. Something was telling me that this was not going to end well. My heart was racing, I could almost hear it banging my ribcage, but I breathed in to contain my panic. I crawled on the ground without a sense of direction. I needed to find a place to hide.

I kept on crawling. My hands scratching the ground while my knees were hurting but I didn't bother to stop. The fog was giving me a hard time let alone I had no idea where I was going. I stopped and looked at my back but all I saw was flashes from the fog while figures moved swiftly that my eyes couldn't figure out who or what it was. I continued to crawl as the adrenaline kicked in. Finally, the fog became thinner as I went forward, and this gave me relief. A few more distance and I was already heaving. The fog disintegrated from this side of the groves and I emerged from the trees beside the stream. I was catching my breath, my knees scraped with dirt and so were my hands. Immediately I stood up, my body was shaking with fear. I turned around cautiously to see if I'd been followed. I wasn't, I was left alone again. My shoulder sagged as I managed to relax. The noises were gone and all I heard was the sparkling sound from the stream. The water looked clean and fresh and suddenly, I wanted to plunge into it to get rid of the dirt in my body. Before I succumbed to easing myself, gunfire shattered the silence and my heart leaped as reflex, followed by another one and it was getting closer. My body tensed and I gave way to panic. I needed to cross the stream right away. I didn't want to be engulfed in a fog once again and so I made the decision out of fear. I jumped off the stream and my feet broke into the cold water. I shivered by the effect of the icy water on my skin, but I didn't have time to analyze what I was feeling. The cold was numbing, and I needed to move fast before the coldness paralyzed me. I moved my feet one at a time. Luck was on my side and I was grateful because the water was shallow, and the current was manageable. I kept on moving and I was almost on the other side. The noises were louder, and the sound of the gunfire made me dizzy but I kept moving my feet forward. My knees were weakened by the fatigue and I felt really tired, but this wasn't the time to stop. I was almost there. Then an inhuman shrieking made me looked back. What I saw from the other side of the stream made me stopped and went rigid. The coldness of the water consumed my entire body that I could no longer move. My eyes bulged in shock and my mouth was caught in mid scream. The creature that materialized from the black smoke was horror personified, it was a demon. So, this was what Olga called darkling. It was beyond my human brain could comprehend as if the thing that was standing on the other side defies the natural laws of the universe. The creature was looking back at me. It stood taller than regular human being, seven feet or even taller. Its red eyes gleamed, signifying death. Mouth opened showing deadly fangs sharper than blade. Skin black as granite and wings spreading behind it the color of dusk. Every beat of its wings produced a midnight smoke spreading everywhere. Nauseated feeling rose from my gut and I felt dizzy. I needed to remind myself that this wasn't the best time to faint. Not when there was a creature ready to slush my throat with its deadly teeth. My eyes were fixed on the creature and the smoke was spreading rapidly that it was now beginning to cross the stream. I couldn't be a sitting duck, I willed myself to move. Thank God my body followed the desperate pleading of my heart. I moved backward using the heel of my feet to balance myself. My eyes were still pinned at the creature which was now walking back and forth as if trying to decide. Finally, I reached the other side of the stream and sighed heavily with my little success. The creature stopped pacing and looked back at me, suddenly it released an awful shriek that made me covered my ears. Its wings beat furiously releasing more dark smokes that was now rapidly crossing the water. I stepped backward to brace myself, but the smokes didn't reach the other side of the stream. I was convinced that the smoke would devour me entirely, yet it bounced back as if hitting an imaginary wall. I gasped with relief and I could even taste the tears streaming down my face. The demon growled in frustration; its wings folded behind its back. It stood there staring back at me, red eyes taunting. I was beginning to breathe evenly while my mind was processing the truth about what I was seeing. It was a demon, they were real.

The creature stood rolling its shoulders and straightening its body, its wings unfolded and started to beat behind it. In an instance that nearly took my breath away, with the sharpness of my eyes had become, I swore that I saw its face gave way to a sinister smile. I covered my mouth as I saw its wings beat driving the creature upward as the dark smokes trailed along before it dissolved into a fume of mist away into the night.

Olga came out of the woods panting. Her chest heaving as she crossed the stream to where I was standing. I could tell that she was happy to see me unscathed. She walked gently as if the cold water didn't bother her. With a gun pointing sideward and a sword dripping with black liquid. When she was near enough, I saw the same black liquid splattered all over her body, but she wasn't bothered by it. She grinned at me as if what happened in the groves was just a game and I felt suddenly intimidated. She could kick some demon's ass when all I did was run and hide.

"Hello there!" She greeted.

"Hi!" I said lamely.

"You've made it." Her smile widened. "I didn't think you'll make it out un-sired. They always make sure that they get the soul they want. They'd been getting most of it lately." She eyed me with amazement.

I stared at her confused. What did the Darklings possibly want? The mere sight of them immobilized me in horror, what more to even stand before one of them, to even near them - that would drive me out of my wit.

"Why? What do they want from me?" I asked in whisper. The thought of the Darklings scared me to death.

"To sire you." Olga said frankly. Her voice was flat and unapologetic. "So, you can breed the next Darkling." She walked past me, and I turned around to stand behind her. I was waiting for her to continue. "Generally, the Demons entire populations are male, and they don't have the ability to procreate. They need a female soul to carry their offspring." She turned around to face me, her eyes glaring filled with anger. "That's what they do to us Lola. Every female who crossover this plain is a game of tug of war. Us, the Guardian and them, the Darkling demons. This has been happening for all of eternity, since the beginning of time. That's the reason why the Guardian existed; it's our responsibility to save the souls, especially the female souls. It is important that we must be there first when someone crossover, or else, they'll suffer a doomed existence in hell. No one in existence deserves to be there, not when there is a chance for redemption." Her gaze lingered, her emerald eyes were deep and drowning. I managed to swallow my fear and the next time I opened my eyes, her stares shifted. Someone caught her attention and that someone was standing behind me.

"You're late." Olga chortled. "What took you so long?"

"Well, I didn't think you'll ever need me here. You've saved one soul yourself." A sound of a male voice caught my ear, deep and husky. I turned around to see who he was. He came out from the woods out of nowhere. I didn't even notice he was there; my new keen hearing didn't hear his footfall. He was tall but not taller than

Seb Whyte, probably an inch smaller but tall enough for a guy. He looked young probably around my age, with a pale complexion, black eyes were cold caught mine. I lowered my gaze for a moment and looked again. Hair black as coal, lips registered a steely grin. He was lean and perfectly clad with black leather outfit resembling Olga. It was probably a guardian thing.

He walked briskly towards us; his grin widened into a smile. "Look who we got here?" He was looking at me. I swallowed when I saw him stood a few feet away from me. This guy is good looking, in a bad boy kind of way.

"This is Lola, they almost got her but I'm glad that they didn't." Olga said.

"I'm Keenan." The guy introduced himself extending a hand to shake mine. I slowly held my hand, embarrassed of how dirty it was from crawling earlier. Keenan gripped my hand and squeeze it gently before releasing. He was wearing gloves so technically our skin didn't touch. But his grip was strong and determine and for the first time in an hour out here I felt safe. His mischievous gaze made me uncomfortable.

"We better go." Olga interrupted. "It's getting dark and the woods can't be trusted at night." She walked past us.

"Wait!" I squirmed. "That thing, they could have got me... but it didn't. I mean the smoke bounced back. It tried to cross the stream, but it couldn't get through..." I explained. I was facing Olga begging for answers. Olga and Keenan exchanged glances at each other, but it was Keenan who spoke first.

"The Demons can't get cross to the stream because this side is a hallowed ground. Lucky for you, you've found and crossed the boundary between the hollowed and the forsaken plain. That stream over there is the borderline." He said and drew his lips in a thin line telling me that I just got lucky.

"Come on. We better go. We need to reach the wall before nightfall." Olga said. She started walking to the woods and taking the lead. Keenan waited for me to go first and so I followed Olga while he trailed behind.

"Where are we going?" I asked. We entered some semi dense groves again and I couldn't help feeling agitated even if I knew that this was a hallowed ground.

"You'll see... Just keep walking. We'll get there in time." Olga answered.

I was aware of the pair of eyes staring behind me, steely as a wolf clawing at my back. His presence drawing me in, I could sense it. Keenan, there was something about him, like a space unfathomable as darkness itself. A part of me was telling me to fear him but a part of me wanted to get to know him. He wasn't Seb, Seb whose eyes filled with life, smile radiant as the sunlight. Keenan was the shadow behind it, the moonbeam at night. I thought about Seb, I thought about the last time I was with him. That was days ago that seemed eternity. Would I ever have a chance to be with him again? Now that I'm dead, would there still be hope for us? Did he cry when he found out about my sudden misfortune? Did he have any remorse? My mind was filled with all this silly nonsense. Of course, he must have felt something. I knew for a fact that there was something special between us. It's sad to say that we would never know the end of it. How about my parents, my brother Ram? How were they coping? I missed them so much. Sadness hit me like a bullet and my current situation finally dawn on me. I am dead. All that I ever work hard for... would be all for nothing. My heart ached as my eyes gave way to tears. If not with the hands gripping both of my shoulders, I wouldn't know that I was already standing rigid staring at nothing.

"Lola, Lola ... you okay? Lola!" His voice was pounding in my head, breaking me out of my sentiments.

"She was in shock." A female's voice. "Just keep calling her."

"Lola, can you hear me?" It was him again.

A pair of black eyes was staring straight at me. Brows furrowed and lips pulled together showing how concerned he was. A hair fell from his forehead that he immediately blew it on the side of his face. His pale skin shone.

"I'm dead." I said. My eyes filled with tears as my voice broke. I succumbed to the dreadful anguish of the dead. Loneliness, sadness, regret, all of it hit me at once. I felt weakened but Keenan held me still. He became my stronghold because my strength left me a while ago.

"It's okay. You'll get through this." It was Olga. "You'll deal with the grief of your death as we all do then you'll learn to accept it sooner." Her voice was sympathetic.

She was sorry for me. All of them were sorry for me because I died, and I couldn't do anything about it. And now I'm in Purgatory, fighting for my life. I just got away from the demon that wanted to sire me. How inviting was that?

I never had an emotional breakdown. This was the first; ironically, it took an afterlife for me to do it. When I finally got to my senses, I noticed that Olga was holding my left arm while Keenan was on my right. We were trailing a narrowed path with a swamp covered in mist on both sides. We were heading to an open bridge made of bricks and stone with angel statues standing in both sides holding a sword. Their wings folded behind their back. On the other side were walls taller than the Great Wall of China. Humongous was an understatement to describe this wall. It stood looming over us, piercing at the sky. With this colossal marvel blocking the last light of the sun, shadows from the wall crept through the nearest waters down to the distant land, altering the air to a deadly cold.

"Welcome to Iduri City." Keenan said.

Chapter 5

I woke up in a small room with a single bed and a squared window covered with thin fabric. Darkness flooded the small corners and I didn't know what time it was. I must have lost consciousness because I didn't know how I got here and worst, I didn't know where I was. The last thing I remember was the sight of clouds covering the top of the giant citadel and that was it. I sat up and let my feet touched the concrete floor. It was cold beneath my bare skin but manageable. I stood up slowly, planting the sole of my feet calculating my strength. I was bracing for the odd feeling of dizziness, but it didn't come. I must have slept soundlessly for hours for it had cured the exhaustion that I had been feeling since the first time I got here. I didn't know dying would take so much of my strength in the afterlife. But I was feeling better now, not a hundred percent but good enough. There was a thin light seeping through the window from the outside, so I walked slowly towards it and peeked. Cold air brushed my face the moment I put the curtain aside. But I realized that it wasn't a curtain to begin with, it's a worn-out fabric cut in half of what used to be a blanket. The cold breeze on my face refreshed me, allowing my pores to breathe and released the stress. I closed my eyes and inhaled deeply to fill my lungs with air and exhaled it along with a satisfying sigh. When I opened my eyes, I saw the moon hanging closely above the sky. Myriad stars splattered across the horizon, sparkling diamond against the dark. I stepped closer to the window and leaned forward on the edge to peruse further. I found out that I was in a building, tenth or fifteenth floor, I wasn't sure. My eyes surveyed the surrounding and despite of the darkness, the moon shone closely shedding us her divine light that made me see rooftops, maze like alleyways and building structures downstairs. My gaze looked horizontally in front of me and farther ahead I saw it once again, the massive wall that enclosed this semi urban jungle, dividing the consecrated ground from the forsaken land.

"Beautiful isn't it?" I turned around to see Olga standing on the doorway holding a candelabrum with three candle lights flickering. She walked to close the gap between us and stood next to me facing the window. Her eyes took the deeper shade of green from the dim light as she gazed out into the night.

"Where am I?" I asked.

"You're in the holy city of Iduri, consecrated by God himself to hold souls that are waiting to be judge before they travel to the next realm." She paused and took a deep breath before continuing. "This entire city is under the protection of the Archangel Raphael, the healer of the Lord, watcher of the East, Prince of the Cherubim." She looked at me and allowed the knowledge to sink in.

"Archangel? You mean the angels are real?" My eyes filled with amazement while my heart leaped with excitement. Olga smiled to see the surprised look on my face before she answered.

"Yes, they are real... and so is God." She said.

"And so are the demons." I murmured.

"Unfortunately, yes... so are the demons." Her lips pulled together as if she was sorry about the truth about the demons.

I looked down and stared at my hands, it looked whiter than it used to. Probably this was normal when you died - as life left you, your skin would turn white to signify the absence of the warmness of being alive.

"What is it Lola?" Olga asked. She was concerned with the sudden changes in my face.

"So, am I really dead?" I was afraid to confirm the truth to myself. It felt weird to accept the reality of being dead. I couldn't just embrace it. I wanted to be alive again, to be part of the living world and breathed the living air.

"I know this is hard for you as it always is for everyone else. But sooner you accept the truth, the sooner you can move on. I can't promise you anything. I will not tell you that it'll going to be easy because it's not. Iduri City is the Purgatory. We are in the lowest realm in the afterlife. Every soul here is waiting for a higher purpose and that alone isn't easy." She turned and paced back to the room and left me standing in front of the window. She placed the candelabrum on the only table in the room, walked a few steps and sat on the bed. I was thinking about my own predicament and when my eyes met hers, she beckoned for me to sit beside her on the bed and so I fallowed.

"How did you die? If you don't mind me asking." She asked.

"Car accident." I said outright.

She thought about it for a while before she spoke again. "You see, most of the souls who have died in tragedy, were the one who found it hard to crossover." She looked at me then looked away as she continued. "The reason for this varies. Some of them rejected the idea of being dead. They believed that they are still part of the living world and choose to linger in Idmuria or earth as you know it, for quiet sometimes. They are the rogue souls, ghosts, phantoms - they roomed Idmuria until they are consumed with madness. Some of them continue to exist while others just ceased in oblivion. Some souls didn't know that they're dead and it takes time and patience to convince them of their fate. But we can help them crossover. They are the most distraught souls that we need to send them to the Limbo Infirmary to heal." Olga's eyes flickered and the next time I met her gaze, she was smiling. "But of course, there are those who were exception to the rules." She said.

"Exception?"

"Yes, and you are the perfect example of it." She said. "After you died your soul crossover to the afterlife right away. Your physical body might still be alive when you left it, but it was as good as being dead because a body cannot survive without its soul."

I stared at her in amazement. My mind was processing all the information she told me. If Olga was telling me this to make me feel better, well, it's not working. I'm still dead and stuck in purgatory and...

"Wait. If I didn't crossover and my body was still alive like you said, could I still go back inside?" I asked.

"No."

"Why not?"

"Because your time has come Lola." She said sympathetically.

"And I don't have a say over it?" I felt anger rising within me. "It's my life! This isn't my choice!" I could feel tears streaming down my face. Olga reached out to touch me, but I stood up immediately and paced the room. "Don't you think it's fair if I was given the choice? Or a head's up perhaps?" My emotions poured out and there was no stopping it. I cried and I no longer cared how I look. It no longer matters if I was wailing like a child. I was dead; someone should give me a break.

"Who made these rules anyway? Tell me!" My shoulders were heaving furiously as I let my sentiments out.

Olga was staring at me silently, but she didn't impede my sudden outburst. I felt sorry for her that she had to witness me looking like a drama queen. My face was soaked with tears and my heart was hurting that all I could do for the moment was cried. Olga approached and opened her arms for me and like a little sister; I accepted her kindness and melted my sorrows in her arms. Her embrace was warmed and gentle, just what I needed to ease the pain. I thought about my mother and the thought of not seeing her again and not being able to hug her crushed me. My mother wasn't here and so I had to accept whoever was available for me and I was grateful for Olga.

"There must be a reason why you're here Lola. We can't just rely on luck that you are an exception. Because I must tell you this... The last soul who bypassed the process and went straight to Purgatory after a horrible death was...me." Olga confessed. "And that was a long long time ago."

I untangled myself from her embrace. The tears subsided but my face was still damp from crying. My eyes met Olga's and I saw that she was tortured by the memories of her lost life. She missed being alive. Her eyes deepened showing the hidden pain. She turned around and walked back to the window and gazed at the stars. She was trying to conceal her agony, but it was already too late for her eyes poured like water in a stream. It flowed unstoppably. I knew that she was still haunted by the tragedy of her own death. I wondered how she died. I wanted to ask her, but I decided to shut my mouth and didn't say a word. Eventually I would learn her story but not today for it wasn't the right time.

She spun around to face me and the tortured soul I saw a while ago was no longer there. How could she conceal it completely?

"You must go back to sleep." She said. "It's still midnight and your body need rest." She paced back to where the table was located and picked up the candelabrum. She was on her way to the door but before she left, I managed to utter the words...

"Thank you." I whispered.

She looked at me; a smile coiled in her lips and gently gave me a nod to acknowledge my gratitude.

"We will talk in the morning. Now, sleep." She left the room. Taking the only light with her, leaving me in complete darkness.

I climbed back to bed and in sadness I coiled in a fetal position. Tears started to fall from my eyes again and I didn't do anything to stop it. I was grieving for my lost life. I wondered when this would end, the grieving part. My mind drifted and I thought about all the people that I cared for... My mom and dad, my brother Ram, Seb Whyte and my best friend Martin Frey. It could have been easier for me to deal all of this if Martin was here; he could bring color to this new world that I was in. I thought about home and school and Rose my car...The truck driver who was still alive and I wasn't. I thought about all of them until my mind was drowsy and tired... Then there was nothing.

Chapter 6

The red dawn approached. When I opened my eyes, a fainted light from the outside altered the temperature in the room. It was morning and I noticed that the curtain had been put back in place and I assumed that Olga came back while I was asleep. I sat up and stretched my arms before I managed to stand. I walked to the window and put the curtain aside to allow the sun. For a distinct moment I found myself drenched with light and the warmth of the sun embraced me with full vigor. I was fully awake as I sulked myself in the fiery glow of the sun; a morning in Purgatory signifies the start of a new day just like in all the worlds. I squinted my eyes to see the horizon clearly. Birds flew in clustered governing the cloudless sky, mist dispersing outside the wall showing the pathway to the groves. From my viewpoint, I saw bricked houses varied in sizes. Most of these concrete houses have similar squared windows. There were cobblestone streets and empty courtyards. So this was Iduri City, a sort of dilapidated version of old Jerusalem. Below me I saw the alleyways filled with movement and hubbub that I could hardly understand. I focused on the noises and I heard souls chattering in variation of languages. I was amazed how they were able to converse with each other despite of language barrier. Most of them were talking in different tongues at each other and managed the conversation well. I concluded that souls are linguists by nature.

A knock from the door disrupted me from my perusing of the city. I spun around to see a pale looking guy, black hair and eyes standing in the door watching me. He was sporting a grin in his face.

"Hi." He said.

"Hey." I responded and wrapped my arms around my body.

"Did you sleep well?" He entered the room and closed the door. I leaned my lower back on the window.

"I think so..." I answered.

"Good. Because you fainted yesterday. You must be very tired." He said as he paced the room and stopped in front of me... He lowered his gaze to meet mine while lips pulled together.

"I guess so... You're..."

"I am Keenan. We met yesterday in case you forget." He smiled

"I... I didn't forget." I stuttered.

"Right. Hungry?" The moment he said it I felt my stomach grumbled in response to his question. My hands covered it reflexively and nodded at Keenan whose smiles widened.

"Well, come on then. Breakfast is served and everybody was waiting for you downstairs." He side stepped to allow me to go first.

"Everybody?" I asked. I was so preoccupied with my own problems that I didn't thought about the other souls living in this building nor did I consider that there were any.

"Yes. The other Guardians. You're in the Zion headquarter, the main office of the Guardianship in Iduri. Right now, you're in the safest place in the realm." He explained proudly and I stared at him like a petrified lamb. He must have sensed my hesitation.

"Don't worry. They're cool and they want to meet you." He said reassuring.

"They do?" I was skeptical.

"Of course, they do. Come." He said encouragingly. "I'll be with you."

Zion Headquarter for Guardianship was housed in a ten-floor story old building at the center of Iduri City. The hallway to the elevator was dark and the wallpapers were dithering while other wall coverings were stripped with decay that all I saw was grey cement. Keenan walked beside me in silence until we reached the elevator. The machine groaned and the door opened. He gestured for me to enter first and then he followed. I saw him pressed the ground button and the elevator groaned once again as it closed. The top of the elevator door showed that we were on the tenth floor. When the machine started to descend, I held my breath for a while, bracing for the worst elevator ride of my afterlife. But the elevator descended smoothly with just a few bumps. I relaxed. My shoulders fell as I stared at Keenan's back as he stood in front of me. Finally, we made it on the ground safe and the elevator groaned as it opened. He stepped out and I followed him.

"We're here." He said.

"So, this is the Guardians headquarter?" My voice was flat; obviously I wasn't impressed with what I saw. I was expecting to see headquarter, a real one like what I saw in movies or at the police station. But the ground floor of the Zion Headquarter was nothing like those. It was more of like an abandoned lobby of a hotel in downtown Silent Hills. This place was deteriorating but what should I expect? I was in Purgatory, the lowest part of the realm as what Olga told me. There was no partition here; all walls have been put down to give way for the training ground or sort of. There was a reception area near the entrance comprises of a table and a chair and nothing else. My eyes wandered and I could see both ends. I looked down to see the worn-out matted floor which the original color was no longer distinguishable. Now I was beginning to see a ground parking lot instead of a lobby.

"It isn't that much I know." Keenan chuckled.

"Well... Not my idea of headquarter." I said.

"This is where we do the drill before we send out the batches for the major posts." He said as we walked towards the center.

"What do you mean?" I asked confused.

"Do you see anyone?" He asked.

I turned around to cover all corners and suddenly realizing what I hadn't noticed earlier that despite how vast this place was, there was no one in here except me and Keenan. My brows shoot up asking.

"Where's everybody?" I asked. My mind was considering the possibility that Keenan was playing tricks on me.

"The base is situated underground." His eyes surveyed the entire vicinity. "We're at the surface. Come, follow me." He didn't wait for me to say anything, he glided towards the center in few strides and I sprinted so I could catch up.

"Where are you taking me?" My voice was louder this time.

"To meet the others"

"And where exactly is that?" I was already feeling irritated. Why couldn't he just tell me where Olga was or the others?

Finally, he stopped walking and spun around to face me. His charcoal eyes lit up as he stood waiting for me to catch up. My brows furrowed showing how annoyed I was.

"Here." He said amused.

"Here, where?" I snapped. "Look, just tell me where it is okay. Enough with the suspense."

I knew that he was mocking me. As if my current desperation amused him. I could see that in his face, his lips pulled together trying to hold a laugh. But he didn't say a word; he just stared taunting my nerve. This guy was impossible, I thought.

"We're here" He said it again and stamped a foot on the floor twice like a child throwing a tantrum. He smiled at me as we waited. I sneered at him. It took a minute before the floor shook beneath us and I panicked. My eyes darted toward Keenan who was currently grinning at me unperturbed. For a moment I thought that the building would collapse, and the bastard just stood there watching me looking like a tool. I wanted to strangle him and stabbed him a hundred times. Then the most insane thing happened. A hole appeared on the floor out of nowhere. It gave way to a spiraled stair equipped with iron railing snaking downstairs.

"What the..." I bit my tongue trying not to swear.

"After you..." Keenan said half smiling.

I recovered from the shock. When I saw Keenan's mocking face, I rolled my eyes and tried very hard to compose myself. With head held high I stepped on the stairs and climbed down while his annoying gaze followed. I was already halfway down when I heard his steps behind. When I reached downstairs, I stopped. I found myself standing at the end of a long hallway. There were life size angel statues standing on each side, lining all the way to the other end. Wings folded behind them. They were geared up in battle outfit but instead of holding a sword, they were holding torches blazed with fire and illuminating the entire place. My eyes were huge, and my mouth was opened, I was amazed with what I saw that I didn't notice someone approaching.

"Hi!" A female voice greeted. When my eyes found her, she gave me a sly smile as she waited for me to recover. Suddenly I felt embarrassed that she caught me looking like a fish with my mouth opened. I struggled to find my voice.

"Hi" I greeted back.

She was a petite looking girl, blue eyes that looked so big in her small heart face, dark blonde hair pulled in a tight ponytail. She looked so young; I wondered how old she was when she died. Her face beamed in excitement to see me. Perfect teeth glinted in front of me, she was pretty. Her voice tingled like bell when she spoke.

"You must be Lola?" She asked.

"Yeah... ahmm..."

Keenan appeared on my side, I almost forgot that he was behind me a while ago. I faced him waiting for a good introduction.

"Lola, Safa - Safa, Lola" That's all he got. What a jerk.

I faced Safa whose smile turned into grin while her eyes shifted at Keenan. She pouted her lips as if thinking what to say. Now I was convinced that she died very young, probably twelve or thirteen.

"What took you so long to fetch her?" Safa asked. "Olga asked you an hour ago."

Keenan smirked and walked past her. She turned around and started walking beside him. I trailed off behind them at the middle. We were now walking in the angel hallway and my eyes wandered again to see the angel statues clearly. They looked grotesque yet beautiful in appearance. These effigies were probably seven feet tall and I wondered if this was really how they look in person.

"We take a tour at the surface before we come here." Keenan said. "I want her to take the stairs instead of the elevator. I think it would be fun. You should see her reaction when the stairs appeared." He chuckled.

"Wait!" I stopped walking. "You mean you did that on purpose?" I was furious. Why did he have to do that? I was already eating by now considering how hungry I was if we didn't make a side tripped at the surface for the purposed of Keenan's theatricality.

Keenan and Safa turned around to face me and saw my face red with anger. I really felt sorry for Safa for seeing my bad side. I couldn't blame myself either for exploding like that, I was hungry as hell. I knew that Keenan was just trying to be nice but right now, my stomach was overthrowing logic.

"Hey, I didn't mean to upset you." Keenan said; I saw the shock on his face that made me winced, in check with my emotion. "I just wanted to tour you around. I'm sorry." His forehead wrinkled.

Safa stood stupefied beside him as if she had no idea what was going on. Her eyes darted from me to Keenan and back and forth. It wasn't fair to throw this all on Keenan, he was just trying to be nice, though annoying but it wasn't his fault. I was still upset with my death and I needed to control this before I could offend anyone. Thank God we were saved by Olga. She appeared quietly behind Keenan and Safa with hands entwined in front of her. There was a questioning look in her eyes, sensing the tension arising in the hallway.

"Is everything okay?" She asked.

Her query was answered by awkward silence. I took a deep breath to relax my nerve and lowered my gaze to the floor to avoid Keenan's stares. I was relieved when a girl's voice broke the silence.

"We're fine." Safa said, managing a smile. "You just save them from having lovers quarrel." She turned around and left.

"We aren't..." I wanted to say that Keenan and I weren't lovers, we barely knew each other but Safa was gone. My eyes met Olgas and I could see that she was amused by the situation. Keenan was silent beside her.

"She's a day-old soul and you're already having trouble controlling yourself not to annoy her?" Olga said directly to Keenan. She wasn't mad at all and I could sense that she was used to his annoying behavior.

Keenan was still staring at me. His charcoal eyes deepened as he narrowed his gazed before he faced Olga.

"I didn't do anything. I was just trying to tour her around." He said.

"Or scare her..." Olga rebutted.

"Whatever..." He started walking in the hallway away from us; his shoulders were high and proud showing his arrogant side. He didn't bother to look back. At the end of the hallway he turned left and disappeared completely leaving me with Olga. She turned to faced me and gave me a sympathetic smile. She reached out and put an arm around my shoulders and urged me to walk with her.

"He's not always like that. He could be a pain in the ass but his one of the best guardians that we have..." She said.

I didn't say anything to oppose Olga. All I did was listened to her speak as she guided me to this dimmed lighted antechamber. We walked a few steps until we reached the end of the hallway and stopped in front of one of the most majestic statues of angel I beheld in my entire existence. The statue was huge, bigger than those that were guarding in the hallway. He, I assumed was a male because of his masculine physicality, stood in alabaster whiteness at the center facing the entrance from where we came. Why didn't I notice this earlier? I thought. The commanding angel was also in battle garb but the breastplate and shield adorning him were made of gold, equipped with massive sword hanging on his side. His right hand was holding a golden staff with twin serpents entwined around the middle to the top where both snake heads were facing each other. Huge wings spread behind the angel's back as if caught in mid-flight, casting shadow over us. The angel's face looked serene yet cunning. His eyes were looking straight to the room as if surveying the world, vigilant of the cruelty among mankind. Something sparked within me as I stared in awe at the angel's face. I knew who he was. I read about him from books and scriptures and from the bible reading at school. There were lots of replicas of him in many churches all over the world. I knew who he was... He was not an ordinary angel; he was one of the pillars of God. This was just a representation of him. It wasn't the real one yet the presence of the statue edicts the authority of the ethereal being. I suddenly had the urge to bow my head - not because I wanted to... but it was the right thing to do, to surrender, in humility to the might of the Archangel Raphael.

My eyes were clouded with tears with the sight of him. I felt peace inside of me, relieving me from all the worries in my mind. My heart beats with unquenchable gladness that made me wanted to burst out laughing. I heard hymn of praises humming in the air and in a moment I wanted to sing a verse and filled my mind with cherubic singing. It was euphoric to say the least and I wanted to stay this way forever. But an arm around my shoulders disrupted me from the blessed trance. A touch so soft and kind that could only belong to Olga. The next time I looked at the angel's face, I swore that I saw it smiled at me and I smiled back. Olga understood what had occurred.

She probably brought me here on purpose because she knew that the Patron of Zion would help me healed the wounds inflicted in me by my death. It worked perfectly well... As I looked deep inside of me, I felt calm, the kind of calmness that gave way to acceptance and later... love.

My soul was healed.

Chapter 7

The feast was held in a spacious chamber. The room also served as the headquarters' cafeteria where Guardians took their meals and rendezvous before and after a long day of scouting for souls to save. There were long tables and chairs arranged apart from each other. We entered at the front door and I saw torches everywhere that lightened and warmed the entire room. Guardians occupied most of the table nearing the front while others were clustered in groups at the back. All of them were busy talking and laughing while feasting on their foods. They didn't notice us coming and I was relieved by this as I didn't want to be the center of attention. I did what I do best, my eyes wandered around. There were paintings of the archangel on walls depicting his role as the almighty's healer and a commander in battle. Some paintings showing the archangel in flight - a beacon of light in the sky, leading his angel armies in heavenly war. Other paintings emphasizing his compassion for the sick souls - healing them and giving them hope. I wanted to see each painting, but I decided to do that some other time. At the front, I saw the biggest portrait of Raphael plastered on the wall. This painting resembled the statue outside. The only difference was the portrait showed his wings folded neatly behind his back, right hand holding a staff while the left hand was carrying what sort of an emerald stone. The object was circle in shape and the green color was vibrant. I stopped and faced Olga to ask what the archangel was holding in the painting.

"It was the healing salve." She said. "The color of green represents him for it was the color of healing and nature."

"So, does he carry it all the time? The healing salve I mean" I asked curiously.

"That is a very good question Lola, but before I attend to your query, you need to eat first." She said. "You must be very hungry by now?" a glint in her eyes as she asked.

I heard my stomach answered and I smiled sheepishly at her. She grinned and ushered me ahead. The table on the right beside a door that probably leads to the kitchen was where we were heading. What I saw made my mouth watered. On the table, there were varieties of food display that gave me the impression of a medieval period version of eat-all-you-can food buffet. My eyes lightened with surprise as if it was the first time, I saw a buffet and I was so hungry that I could lunge at the table and eat everything. But of course, I held myself back as I didn't want everyone thinking that I was crazy. My mind was so focused on my hunger and my eyes were fixed on the table, salivating over the food like a mad dog that I failed to notice how silent the room had become. I looked around and saw all eyes were on me. Most of the Guardians stopped what they were doing; some stared with blank faces probably wondering who I was. Not to mention that I was caught in the most embarrassing moment of trying to attack their banquet food. My eyes wandered looking for exit. I thought about the door beside the table but I wasn't sure where that leads me, so I unchecked that option, how about hiding under the table? No, I won't consider that. I was trapped and everyone was closing in with curiosity in their stead. The room suddenly felt small with these eyes staring and questioning. My face was burning with embarrassment that I'd rather preferred those mean gossip girls from school rather than the vehement scrutiny of the Guardians. These eyes weren't just looking at me, they're seeing through my soul and I never felt so exposed as if standing naked in front of them. All Guardians were geared up in black leather pants and boots, even the women were clad in combat outfit and stood equal with men, their white faces severed and beautiful. As my eyes surveyed, I noticed that everyone looked different from each other, yet they were brothers and sisters. An explosion of nationality was the best way to describe it. By this, I concluded that religion and race didn't really matter anymore when you die. Here in Purgatory, you'll dwell in the realm that considers only one thread. This thread serves only one purpose and that is to help all souls ascend to the next realm. But this was within the city gate, outside the walls of Iduri, the rule changed. Finally, a familiar face emerged from the crowd, Safa, her petite formed sashayed to the front line, a faint smile on her lips. I smiled back.

"Guardians!" Olga's voice was loud and commanding, bouncing within the four corners of the wall. It dawned on me that she held the highest position as she stood in authority among them. She was their leader, and everybody listened to her but she also cared for each of them. I could feel the maternal instinct from the way she looked at them like these Guardians were her children. A bond so deep that cannot be conquered.

"I would like you to meet someone. For those who already heard what happened yesterday, you must already know this. But I want you all to listen." Her eyes surveyed each of the Guardians face as they listened carefully. "This..." Olga placed a hand on my shoulder while everyone's attention shifted from her to me and immediately, I lowered my gaze to avoid their staring.

"Is Lola Goods. She, crossover yesterday right after she died in an accident." I heard the crowd murmured from each other, but I didn't bring my eyes to look at them. A pang of pain hit me suddenly. Olga's confirmation to the group regarding my death made it more official.

"She is our new recruit." Olga said. I wasn't sure if I heard her correctly as my eyes were fixed at her in disbelief. I thought she was joking, and she didn't mean what she just said. I couldn't be a Guardian; there was nothing in my body that could combat a demon. I didn't think that I could do it. Olga must be mistaken, and I didn't want to disappoint her. But when I met her eyes, I knew that she wasn't joking, she was serious as hell. How did it come to this? I bit my lips to stop me from protesting. There must be a mistake.

When the Guardians heard the news there were murmurs. But I could see that the tension had passed, and every shoulder lowered and relaxed. Some of them moved forward and welcomed me to their group while others gave me an approving nod. All of them were warmed and accepting and I didn't feel any resistance at all. There were those who were puzzled and might doubt my capability to be a Guardian and I understood them because I doubted myself more. Yet later I found them surrendered to the idea of me being one of them. Safa was happy to know this and locked me in a tight embrace. I was touched with her gesture. Then she tagged me along and introduced me to the crowd. I looked back to find Olga, but she was already talking to someone else. I almost forgot how hungry I was, but I still needed Olga's explanation with this surprise announcement as I didn't see this coming.

Finally, I got to eat and I took everything in my plate that I didn't care what other souls would say about my appetite. I chose the table at the center and I was accompanied by Safa most of the time. As I was eating, I wondered where Keenan was. My eyes immediately searched around the cafeteria but there was no sign of him. Safa probably picked up my anxiousness.

"Have you seen Keenan?" I asked her.

"Oh, Keenan huh?" She grinned. "He might be out on the street. He did that all the time, taking time to talk to souls." She said as she took a spoon full of mashed potato. The thing about Safa, you didn't have to ask her anything. She spieled the goes and going inside the building and in a matter of an hour I spent with her, I thought I already knew everyone. I won't consider her a grandstander; she was young and gullible and probably happy to have someone to talk to that was not uptight as the others. I was grateful for her company.

But where was Keenan? I felt horrible for how I treated him earlier and I wanted to apologize. I was hoping that I would bump into him when Safa gave me an intensive tour around the building. But there was no Keenan and I felt disappointed by this and I didn't know why.

"The rooms upstairs are occupied by the Guardians." Safa said as we walked down the corridor. "The operation happens mostly down here. The infirmary is in the room on the left." She said.

The underground base was basically easy to navigate since the structured pattern was on T shape. The main corridor that was heavily guarded with warrior angel statues was where the entrance was located. At the end of the hallway you'll find the majestic statue of the Archangel Raphael, standing in between the right and left wings. On the right wing you'll find the medieval cafeteria and the kitchen. There were training rooms and the shower rooms each for both genders. While on the left you'll find closed door chambers occupied by Guardian leaders, the infirmary, armory and Olga's chamber.

"What floor is your room?" Safa asked.

My eyes were busy wandering around paintings and relics adorning the side of the hall that I failed to hear her questioning. When I met her eyes, she was beaming at me.

"What?"

"I understand how you feel. I was like you when the first time I got here. This place is incredulously amazing." She said looking around. Then her eyes settled back on me. "Wait until you see the entire city."

"Are you going to tour me outside too?" I asked excited.

"Oh no!" Her voice ringing like bells. "I am not that familiar outside the base. Keenan would be the best one to tour you around." Her smile was warmed.

She ushered me to walk along the main hallway and I saw the angel warriors once again. I just realized that all of them were wearing uniform helmet and with long hair. Raphael had a long hair, curly and shoulder length in all his paintings that I saw so far. Safa was silent for a while and I was disturbed by this sudden change in her mood. I didn't know what I had said to silence her. I tilted my head to glance at Safa and saw that she was solemnly contemplating. Hands clamped together in prayer; chin was up while eyes were staring but distant. I suddenly felt worried with her uneasiness.

"Safa..."

"Yes?" She asked blankly.

"Are you okay? You seemed quiet." I said.

"Oh, I'm sorry... I was just..." She stopped walking and faced me. I could see in her eyes that there was something bothering her.

"I hope you don't mind me asking this. Olga said earlier that you died in an accident. Is that true?" her forehead crumpled, worried that I might be offended. I stared at her for a moment before answering. Now that Safa asked, talking about my death was weird but I guessed that I was giving myself a favor by doing this.

"Yes. I died in a car accident." I said then looked away.

Safa stared at me appalled. I could feel that her mind was processing what I just told her. I was glad that I told her about it because saying it out loud won't change a thing but it help me came to terms with my own reality. Safa's silence disturbed me. I wondered what made her asked me about my death or why was the reason of my passing bothered her... I looked back at her.

"How did you die Safa?" I asked.

My question startled her but immediately found her bearing and shifted her attention back to the main hallway. She started walking and I followed. I didn't ask her twice because I knew how hard it was to recollect bad memories. I remember Olga last night and the pain I saw in her eyes. I suddenly realized that in Purgatory, talking about death was the most personal question you could ask to a soul and unless your bond was great, asking about someone else's death story was out of the question.

"I also died in an accident." She confessed. I wanted to ask her how, but I decided not to press her with it. I learned to stay quiet.

"I fell." She stopped and walked again.

"Oh... I'm sorry." I said.

"Don't be... It's okay. I already embraced my fate but... It's been a long time since someone asked me about it." She said smiling slyly.

"Do you still remember how it happened?" I asked.

"I don't think someone will ever forget. It's something you will take to your grave and even to the afterlife. All souls here knew how their lives ended. It's our gift, to remind us that we were once alive. But it's also our torment... A sort of reminder that we could never go back and undo things." She said.

I was dumbfounded listening to Safa. How could someone as young and innocent as Safa knew about torment? I didn't have enough experience in life to know about it myself. But then it dawned on me that I didn't know when she died. She might be in Purgatory for a very long time to witness the hardship of souls.

"I was in a convent." She continued. "I was about to become a nun when I died. It was the only thing that I wanted to be in life, to be in a convent and served God. I was 13-year-old, young and restless and..." She paused, her face was serious as she reminisced. "The rain was hard the night before and I woke up the next morning with the top floor drenched in water that came from the window and flooded the stairs and the stone floor on the ground. Most of the windows were old and needed repairing. The carpenter was commissioned to fix it, but he was out in another village and he was due to come the week after. Since the rain was unexpected, nobody was prepared for it. I remember running from my cell, eager to offer my help to the sister's downstairs to put away the water and clean and dry the stoned floor. It was always like that in the convent. We helped each other to get through the day and we were satisfied with what we had; we didn't need much. I was still wearing my sleeping gown when it happened. I was on my way down hasting and I didn't anticipate how slippery the stairs were." Safa exhaled deeply.

"You slipped." I added.

Safa nodded and I gasped at the infectious pain I saw in her eyes. The same pain I saw in Olga last night. I wanted to hold her and told her it would be fine, but I doubted if she even needed comforting more than I did. I'm glad that Safa told me about how she died even if she didn't have to. I felt like the bond of friendship between us was sealed for eternity. We reached the elevator and Safa pushed a button for it to open. The machine groaned as it opened. Safa took me to the surface and by this time, the surface was busy with Guardians running around. Some of them were huddled in groups and others were simply doing training. Most of these Guardians I already met at the base during breakfast earlier while there were few unfamiliar faces who just probably arrived from a night of patrolling. Safa greeted them while I stood silently behind her. They nodded at me as Safa introduced me as the newbie. There were those who extended their hands to shake mine and I received those handshakes politely. I looked around to find Keenan, hoping he was here but I was disappointed. There was not even a shadow of him.

A loud noise got everyone's attention. A band of Guardians burst inside the surface that made everyone stopped and turned. I saw Safa rolled her eyes as she faces the incoming night patroller. I had this feeling that she knew who they were, and she didn't like them. I moved closer to Safa while my eyes were fixed on the group that just came in. Most of them were huge men, warrior built, tattooed, holding huge guns and swords. They were screaming and laughing as they walked toward us and Safa immediately hold my arm and dragged me to the side to pave the way. My eyes perused them, and they looked brutal and barbaric - the kind of men who kill for fun. Then my eyes drifted to the front and I was surprised that among these beasts who growled literally was a woman. She was clad in Guardian uniform just like everyone else, thick black silky hair, piercing black eyes, pale and rugged. She reminded me of Keenan, the female version. She surveyed the surrounding as she walked among the group. She was the only one who wasn't laughing. She continued to look around as if looking for someone; her eyes were cold and deadly. I made a mistake of staring at her because when her cold eyes met mine, I had a sudden urged to run and hide. I looked down and bowed my head. Her gaze scared the hell out of me. When her group passed us, I tilted my head to take a glimpse of her again but she was surrounded by huge bodies of men blocking her figure. I couldn't see her until they disappeared to take the elevator probably heading to the base.

"Who are they?" I asked, still looking at the elevator.

"The Barbarians." Safa said smirking.

"Barbarians?" I asked.

"That's how they called their platoon." Confusion must be written all over my face that Safa's sly smile turned into a wide grin.

"All of the Guardians belong to a certain platoon. We have 20 platoons in Zion and the Barbarians, they're the first. They are assigned to guard the forbidden road." She said.

"And the girl?" I asked.

Safa sneered, that gave me the idea of how she despised the Barbarian woman.

"She's they're leader. Her name is Sula."

Chapter 8

I woke up early the next morning. The room was cold and dark and all I could hear was my steady breathing. I must be tired from yesterday's activity with Safa that the minute I hit the bed last night, I drifted immediately to sleep. It was dreamless and quiet, I see nothing, but darkness whelmed me in a cocoon. But instead of panic, I felt peace. I wanted to dream about the life I lost but the dream didn't come. The minute I opened my eyes, I tried hard to conjure all the memories that I had when I was still alive. I wanted to embrace those memories once again, but I was troubled that it took me a while to paint a picture of my mother in my mind. Those memories were slipping from my grasp and the dread that I felt was immediate. Something told me that this was normal, that the more the soul stay in the afterlife, everything that defines you as human will be stripped away. You'll be reborn as a soul. Would I be losing all those memories? I couldn't bear the idea of forgetting my family. It was the only thing that I have left. My brother's face appeared in my mind. I saw his green eyes beamed; the freckled in his face, his brown hair - he was a male version of me. Ram's face brought a smile to me and suddenly, the darkness became bearable. I held the thought for a while. It took me a moment to realize that my eyes were wet with tears. I was crying and I didn't even notice it. I wiped the tears with the back of my hand and sat up. The floor was cold against my feet, but it doesn't really matter. I stood up and walked towards the window. It was a moonless night and the stars were distant and reluctantly hiding behind dark clouds. I closed my eyes and breathed deeply, allowing the cold morning air filled my lungs. I opened my eyes as I breathed out and suddenly, I felt awake and my vision was clearer. The darkness outside was unnerving. The walls loomed over the village and casting shadows from the roofs below. Something was brewing from beyond those giant walls and probably it was just my imagination or a hint, but something wasn't right. Then suddenly, an explosion shattered the silence. My eyes darted from the groves outside. The explosion was followed by gunshots. I heard voices screaming from a distance, there were inhuman growls that made the hair in my arms stood. I leaned closer to the window and squinted my eyes to see clearly. There were movements at the alleys beneath the Zion Headquarter. People running clad in black hoods, moving towards the gate. "Guardians" I said.

What's happening? I needed to know what the commotion was all about. Another explosion; this one was closer to the wall. My eyes were huge in shock to see the smoke rising to the sky. I heard voices below. Platoon leaders cascading command as the guardians spread through the alleys moving swiftly in different directions. The door from my room opened in a bang and I jumped in fear to see Safa holding a candle with huge eyes staring back at me.

"Safa! What's happening?" I almost yelled.

"Darklings." She answered. "They never come closer to the wall... Not until now."

I stared at her appalled with my eyes wide and mouth opened. I didn't know what to say or how to react. Safa mirrored my fear and she walked in haste toward me and held my arm.

"Olga told me to get you. She said that the Darklings must be looking for something and..." She stopped and she seemed searching for the right word to say.

"Do you think they're looking for me?" I asked and the thought of it made me shuddered.

"I don't know what to think as of now. We must go to the base. We will be safe there. Olga didn't tell me much. Let's go."

There's no need to argue with the situation. For the first time my mind was blank and all I wanted was to follow Safa to the base downstairs or wherever we could be safe. I know that this wasn't the right attitude for a Guardian. To be one, someone must be fearless and ready to face the enemy or in this case the Darkling demons. I thought about Sula and her platoon of Barbarians. She must be at the front line by now fighting fearlessly. How could I be like her? I was nothing like her. For a Guardian, I must be fraud. Safa and I reached the base and the moment the elevator door opened; I saw chaos. The magic stairs were opened and Guardians where running everywhere. I moved closer to Safa and held her hand to show that I was scared.

She didn't say anything but in response, she squeezed my hand to tell me that everything would be okay. I wasn't convinced by that and my anxiousness was rising inside my body that made me wanted to vomit. With my free hand, I covered my mouth and swallowed hard to stop the bile from my throat and for a minute it worked. Safa pulled me closed to her as we snaked the hallway. I walked behind her to give way for the Guardians hasting for the stairs. When we reached the intersection Safa turned left and I followed. I took a quick glance at the Archangel Statue and made a short prayer for protection. At first, I thought we were heading to see Olga, but we didn't stop at Olga's chamber. I wanted to call Safa in case she forgotten Olga's room but it seemed Safa knew where we were heading and so I followed her without protest. We passed through the infirmary and I could see Guardians lying on beds and it was literally mayhem. At last we stopped in a closed-door room at the end of the left wing. Safa looked at me but didn't say a word and motioned a hand to knock at the door but the door immediately opened and there stood Keenan staring at our frightened faces.

"Keenan." I said.

He looked tired and the dark circles in his eyes were visible against his pale skin. He seemed like he hadn't slept for days. Hair fell in front of his forehead and the tip brushed his thick lashes. But his eyes were like blade as his gaze shifted from Safa to mine. He was wearing the Guardian uniform and I noticed the gun in his right hand.

"Come on in." He said and stepped aside for us to enter his chamber. He closed the door right away the moment we were in. He walked past us to the wooden table at the center of the room. I stared at him, but he didn't acknowledge me, as if I wasn't there. He was still mad at me, that was obvious, and I wanted to apologize but this wasn't the right time for that. I took a note to do it as soon as possible.

"Where is Olga?" I asked. My voice was shaking, and it was apparent how nervous I was. I stood behind him waiting for his answer, but he didn't turn around to address me. He was assembling something from the table and a minute passed before he spun and handed a gun to Safa and then to me. His eyes leveled on me and his stares was cold that froze me from where I stood.

"Olga is at the gate leading all the platoons. She instructed me to keep you safe. No one is going out of this room until I say so..." He said; his voice was terse.

"What is happening Keenan? I don't understand why the Darklings are attacking us." Safa said.

"They'd been planning for an attack for a long time. They're just waiting for the right time, waiting for a reason to do it." His eyes fell back to mine and I shudder. "Now, they have their reason." The moment he said it, he turned around and went to the closet. When he came back, he was holding a Guardian uniform and handed the garb to me. I stared at him as my hand reached out to take it.

"You're one of us now. It's appropriate to wear the right outfit." He said.

For a moment I became conscious about what I was wearing. I was still wearing the flat shoes I wore before I died. I embraced the uniform in front of me and I was looking for a place where I could change. Keenan pointed the bathroom for me, and I didn't wait for him to finish talking, I went straight ahead and closed the bathroom door so I could change and got this over with. I knew it was rude, but he'd been a jerk to me since I entered his chamber. I could almost feel his frustration the moment I locked the door. I smiled with my small triumph. When I got out of the room Keenan and Safa stopped talking and just stared. I gave them a constraint smile and walked toward them. Safa was sitting on the bed and I sat right next to her while Keenan was leaning his back on the wall facing Safa and me. His eyes followed me from the bathroom to the bed. The uneasiness of being watch made me held my breath and knowing that one of those eyes belonged to Keenan made it even worst.

"You look good in it." Safa complimented me.

"Thanks..." At first, I thought the uniform was uncomfortable, but it hugged my body perfectly and I realized that the material was adaptive to the temperature of the environment. The lightness of it made me wanted to run and sprint and jump and do anything physical. I loved my uniform and I traded those doll shoes and worn out clothes I'd been wearing for days now.

"It felt comfortable." I said and brought my eyes to meet Keenan. I didn't know what he was thinking and so I would never know if he approved the uniform on me or not. I held my gaze and I did my best not to flinch. He was the one who withdrew first and in my mind, I celebrated my triumph for the second time. Why do I need his approval in the first place? I looked down.

"Thanks..." I said. But he didn't respond. He was obviously giving me the silent treatment.

When I glanced at him once again, he was playing a knife in his hand. There was something about Keenan that disarmed me. My entire body was telling me to stay away from him but the more I resisted, the more my defiance. There was something about his character that interests me, the danger that he depicted, his being brutal and unapologetic. Despite all those gores, I saw the tamed beast inside of him, the guy who was desperate, longing and craving for good and... love. I saw that in his eyes every time he looked at me.

"How were they able to cross the water?" Safa asked, breaking the awkward silence that passed in the room. My musing about Keenan was thrown out of the window when I realized what Safa meant.

"The stream..." I remembered the dark smokes hitting a sort of invisible walls.

The entire city was a holy place. How did they breach it? Safa was frantic but she was right. If the Darklings could breach a hallowed ground, then what stopping them from attacking the city in full force. Safa and I were looking at Keenan, desperately waiting for answers. He stopped doodling with his knife and stared at our worried faces. His reaction was scolding but I knew that it wasn't directed at us. He was mad about something else.

"The demon born will burn if they tried to breach the shield. Because this place is consecrated, the power of the archangel will never let them pass through. But the Darklings found a way to avert that." His voice was scarred while lips sneered.

"But how?" Safa asked terrified.

"Half-breed." His eyes settled to the unknown. "They'd been abducting souls. They sired female souls for breeding purposes. The ones that are breaching the shield right now are half demons and since the soul is considerably good by nature, it's the one that allowed them to pass through hallowed ground."

"But I thought demons can't conceive? How does the demon born being created?" My naivety almost disarmed Safa and Keenan and they stared at each other before Keenan answered.

"Demons breed from hell Lola and all of the original demons were angel once. Now, other demons born from the darkness of their souls, these are cast away souls who were judged and thrown away because of how evil they were when they're alive. Some of them died and went straight to hell."

"But you said souls are good by nature." I argued.

Keenan looked at me with boredom in his eyes. "There is always the exception."

The bile in my throat made me wanted to throw up and I swallowed hard to prevent it. I leaned forward to put my head in the palm of my hands and stayed there for a while. Safa was quiet beside me and I understood her. The information that Keenan told us was a lot to process and thinking about it made me dizzy. Keenan walked around the bed and sat on the other side paralleled to us. I took a peeked from my fingers and I saw Safa leaned back and lay on the bed in silence. Absentmindedly I followed her and the moment my head hit the bed; tiredness made itself known that I just wanted to lay there for a while. A minute later, Keenan lay in between Safa and me. His head was closer to mine that I could almost hear him breathed. I wanted to turn my head to see him but I stopped myself.

"What should we do?" Safa whispered.

"We have to stay here for a while and wait for Olga. They will have to come back here to regroup." Keenan said.

I turned my head to look at Keenan. He was staring at the ceiling. My eyes traced the outline of his face. His eyes were fixed to the roof unblinking, his narrowed nose pointing proudly, and lips pulled together to form a straight line. He was gorgeous in this angle and his beauty burned in my mind that my eyes were glued at him. His mind was far away, and I couldn't seem to follow the train of his thoughts because he was one of those people I know who was brilliant of hiding their real emotion, suppressed it until it disappeared. But I didn't believe that it would just disappear completely. Those hidden feelings, it might lay dormant inside hiding behind bruised heart but no matter the suppressing, it will push its way to the surface one day, begging to be dealt with.

Caught in deep contemplation, the next time I blinked, my eyes were trapped against abysmal stare. His black eyes pierced through me unabashed without warning. My body tensed in response and I was supposed be offended by this, but I was not, surprisingly. His face was flawless, like a statue devoid by human emotion which was very frustrating. His eyes sparkled like black water, so deep that I almost felt sinking deeper and deeper. I pushed myself to blink to severe the connection between us and moved my head to face the ceiling.

Aloud banging on the doormade the three of us back on our feet. Safa stood beside the bed inching towardthe wall and I huddled beside her. Her hand was so cold when I reached for itand I knew that she was terrified. She had a reason to be terrified for I wascold with fear myself. The thought of those Darklings made me sick. Keenanpulled out the gun and he looked at Safa and me before he moved cautiously tothe door. My hand was clutching Safa so hard I was afraid that I might hurt her,but she didn't move and say a word. When Keenan reached for the door, hecarefully unhinged the lock and opened it. Safa gasped while I struggled to hearthe chaos outside against the loud drumming of my own heart. Keenan's gun waspointed forward, his hand was steady directing the gun to a person standing infront of him. I didn't hear a gunshot and I thought it was a good thing. In aminute I saw Keenan lowered the gun and my heart tamed as my breathing returnedto normal. The fuzzy vision cleared, and I saw that the person standing infront of him was a woman, Sula.

Chapter 9

Keenan stepped aside from the door to accommodate Sula. Her eyes were wild and filled with rage. Her face was contorted with anger, yet still beautiful and grotesque. Her demeanor was tough and intense; I could see the remnant of battle from her. She was strong and proud, and it was obvious that war fed her hunger for violence. She enjoyed killing demons and the act itself consumed her. She stepped forward and stood on the other side of the bed facing us, Keenan was standing behind her. Her gaze traveled back and forth between Safa and me. When our eyes locked, I saw her facial expression hardened. Later did I realize that she was already glaring at me, it made my knees began to wobble. I stared back. I know that I couldn't fight the way she fought, and I couldn't be as good as her in any circumstances, but I couldn't give her the impression that I was weak.

"The wall is secured... for now." She said.

"For now?" Keenan stepped forward.

"Yes brother, for now. They almost made it to the gate; it was almost a victory for them. But we were right on time." She paused. "They would do it again, I'm sure of that."

So, she was Keenan's sister. No wonder the resemblance was so strong. You could cut her hair and the two of them could pass as twins. She was almost as tall as him but though they were probably equal in strength and skills in battle, Keenan knew how to manage his fury and where to point it. Sula, in every beat of her heart, was a bomb waiting to explode.

"Olga will be here any minute now. She just wanted to make sure that everybody is okay. We might have some casualties. All injured Guardians are already at the infirmary." She said and turned around ready to go.

"Where are the other platoons?" Keenan asked.

"My platoon chased the Darklings to the groves while others are scouting outside. We just wanted to make sure that no demons are hiding behind the shadow of the walls." She paused. "Some of them are very sneaky." Her last words before she left.

Keenan waited for her sister to disappear and out of hearing range before instructing us to stay in his chamber. Safa and I nodded, worries were imprinted in our faces, yet he ignored it. He stormed out of the room and I felt empty suddenly now that he wasn't there standing in front of us. I watched the space that he vacated and sighed. Why was I feeling ridiculous about Keenan? The emotion I felt about him was so strong, but I couldn't even decipher what it was about.

"Olga will keep Iduri safe, I'm sure of that. I think the demons will not going to launch another attack anytime soon. We'll be okay." Safa talked mostly to herself. She was looking at a space and was trying to convince herself that everything would turn out fine. Her child like face was optimistic and I felt sorry for her. She walked back to the bed and lied down. I didn't follow her, I stood motionless yet restless inside. I wanted to follow Keenan not because I couldn't stand a minute not being close to him, but I wanted to know exactly what was happening. When my eyes moved back to the bed and saw Safa with her eyes closed, I relaxed. She desperately needed that sleep and I hope she'll feel better when she woke up. Without thinking, I headed to the door and in a minute, I was already walking along the left wing of the base not knowing where to go. I just wanted to leave that room so I could breathe. I thought that if I didn't leave Keenan's chamber, I would faint without enough breathable air to fill my lungs. I walked faster. The entire hallway was a disaster, I saw wounded Guardians carried in stretchers and some of them were placed on the floor in the hallway because the infirmary was already full. The painful screaming was too much but I sucked it in and moved forward. The door from Olga's chamber was slightly opened and I moved closer to check if she was inside. When I reached the door, I heard voices. They were having a meeting inside and I heard intense discussion and cursing. I heard a male voice then a female then another one. I wasn't sure how many people inside, but I guessed there were few. I knew that they were arguing, and I felt bad for doing this, but I inched my ear closer to the door to hear what they were talking about. I didn't get the chance to find out what the buzz because the door opened, and Keenan stood in front of me with huge eyes staring back at me. Yeah! He didn't expect me to be there eavesdropping and from the look in his face, he was taken aback. Just to give you an idea, being caught snooping is embarrassing, I mean for me I kind of wanted to just vanish and disappear in thin air. I wanted to be literally the ghost I knew from the living world - something invisible. It was shameful. I took what was left of my dignity and say "Hi." Shyly.

Keenan didn't reply, he just sorts of stared and skinning me with his eyes which didn't help given my current situation. I lowered my gaze to hide my blushing. I was imagining my face going scarlet, but I wasn't sure if dead people turned red when embarrassed.

"At first I thought Darklings are the sneaky ones. I guess my assumption was wrong. Very wrong." Sula appeared behind Keenan. Her lips formed a sarcastic smile. I didn't say anything in return and bit the inside of my lower lip.

"Come inside Lola." It was Olga.

I bowed my head and entered Olga's chamber. Keenan and Sula stepped aside as I walked past them. I could feel Keenan's eyes watching me seriously. The door closed behind me and I wasn't sure if it was Sula or him. Olga's chamber was spacious, and the ceiling was high. There were huge candles everywhere. The bed was neatly tucked, and I was sure I saw silk in there. I walked slowly to where Olga was and looked up to see her face. There were dark spots in her chin and forehead, and it was all over her arms. It was demon blood; I wrinkled my nose because of the foul smell coming from it. Olga smiled looking at me. She looked tired and I could see it in her eyes and the dark shadows around it. She badly needed a day of undisturbed sleep. Olga aged in just a day and now I understand how a war could change a person literally. But this was Olga, her motherly face was loving and calm and I felt safer around her.

"I'm sorry for the smell. It's bad I know." She said. "Dried Demon blood could make the vultures turn away." Her voice was caring.

She was standing in front of a table; a map was spread on top of it along with candles and quills. It must be the map of the city. Olga asked me to sit in the chair next to the table and I followed. My eyes drifted on the map and she noticed this... She sat in a chair parallel to where I was and suddenly, I realized that there were other souls inside the room aside from Olga and me. Keenan stood behind Olga and Sula next to him. For a moment there was silence, I could almost feel the tension hanging in the air, but nobody dares to break the ice. I surveyed each of their faces and noticed that all eyes were staring back at me. I shifted my weight in the chair to hide my discomfort, but I bit my tongue in order to stay quiet. I met Olga's eyes, she was staring back at me, observing, calculating as if searching for the right words to say. Then her eyes shifted to the table in front of us.

"We've never been attack before; this is the first time." She said with a contained voice. "They were never that daring." She paused. I kept my mouth shut, afraid to interrupt Olga from what she wanted to say. She stared deep into my eyes and this time I held her gaze and didn't back down. "It's obvious that they were looking for someone. The Darklings that attacked the wall were low born half breeds;

they're the only one that could breach the hallowed ground. The high born must be waiting in the grooves."

"Do you think it has something to do with me?" I asked; my voice trembled. Olga didn't answer me right away, she was carefully assessing me. At last she nodded in response.

"But how could you say that? I just got here and..." I was starting to panic, and I was already catching my breath. What did the Darklings want from me? What could they possibly want? I wanted to stand up, but my knees wobbled and decided to stay in my seat. Olga leaned forward; her eyes filled with sympathy towards me; she knew how hard it was for me. I was just a day-old soul. Despite of her motherly persona, I saw the authority inside of her and she would do whatever it took to save the city and the souls the Guardians swore to protect.

"Something happened at the stream when we were attacked yesterday. You said that a Darkling was pursuing you." She said. "You need to tell me exactly what had happened Lola." Olga's face was serious this time.

My eyes shifted from her to Keenan who was standing like a statue behind Olga. His eyes glinted from the candlelight and he gave me an encouraging nod. I turned my attention back to Olga and told her everything that happened with the Darkling that almost got me sired. I told her about the screeching sound and the frustrated growl, I told her that I was convinced that I saw it smiled at me before it took off. I described to Olga how the demon looked like; I gave her a poor estimation on how tall it was. Olga's eyes were steady, but I could see that her mind was processing everything I was telling her.

When I finished telling there was an awful silence in the room, as if everyone was holding their breath.

"You said that the color of the eyes was red?" It was Sula asking. I saw fear that I never expected to see in her face.

I nodded to answer her question. Sula swallowed hard and from there I knew that it wasn't good. I shoot a questioning look to Olga, but I saw her staring at me with mouth slightly opened. I wasn't sure if she was thinking or simply appalled. She blinked and opened her mouth to speak but she was cut by a frantic voice of Sula.

"Agaliarept, it must be him." Sula clenched her teeth as she mentioned the name.

"Sula, we didn't know that yet. We cannot assume that unless we are sure." Olga said strongly.

I was confused watching them. What was that name? I never heard that before. My heart suddenly started to beat faster, and I placed a hand over my chest to control myself. A hand touched my shoulder, warmed and strong. When I looked up, I was shocked to find Keenan. How did he crossed the room so quickly; I didn't notice him walking toward me. He was good at dissolving in shadows and reappearing. His strong grasped on my shoulder gave me courage and despite of the drumming of my heart I found solace knowing that he was there for me.

"Who is Agaliarept?" I asked.

Olga and Sula looked at me, their eyes were huge and unsteady, for the first time I saw fear in them as the mention of the name. I felt silly by doing so but I had no idea. I needed to know. Olga's face recovered and softened. She was calculating as she spoke.

"We don't mention that name in here Lola..." She paused. "Names in Purgatory has power... it could summon the most powerful demon alive." She gave me a sympathetic smile. I kept my silence thinking that Sula mentioned the name first earlier, but I didn't voice it out. "Don't blame yourself because it isn't your fault. It isn't anyone's fault. Assuming Sula is correct, then the city of Iduri is in grave danger because the demon that pursuing you is not an ordinary one. If the name that you have mention is him... we are dealing with the grand general of hell. He is as old as the pit itself for he commands its second legion."

He was a commander of hell, the demon that was pursuing me at the stream yesterday. My last strength crumbled, and tears fell in my eyes like a fountain. My body trembled as my mind absorbed what Olga said. The first demon that I had encountered wasn't just a high born but a General. How lucky was that? I had hell's own bane as my suitor. I was now convinced that life and the hereafter were literally playing tricks on me. Keenan squeezed my shoulder lightly and I thanked him for that because it brought me back to my senses.

"The high lords in hell wouldn't just covet a soul." Sula stepped forward.

"Sula..." Keenan's voice was low.

"Brother, you all knew this." She turned around addressing the Guardians inside Olga's chamber until her gaze fell on me. "They didn't just sire any soul... they only sire souls that are virgin." Her eyes were dark and fierce that made my entire body cold.

Chapter 10

Now I felt ridiculous. So, what if I died a virgin? I shouldn't be punished because of that lame reason alone. I knew that being a virgin in the modern world Idmuria before I died was old fashion because as early as it seemed, girls at school were busy exploring boys the moment they hit freshman year. It was probably the trend but my being a virgin shouldn't be a big deal. I was proud to be labelled as conservative and there was nothing wrong with that. It wasn't a problem of morality; I guessed it was more about finding the right person. The modern girl might be laughing about how lame my excuses were, but I wasn't sorry for it. I wanted my Mr. Right; I was hopeless romantic that way. You must take that from the girl who grew up watching Disney movies. In the afterlife it was totally a different story because right here in purgatory, I was in big trouble and my virginity had everything to do with it. The General of hell was after me for the main reason that high born demons had this crazy preference when it comes to finding their Ms. Right. They only preferred virgin, such as me. Ironically, virgin imports didn't come in bulk orders via FedEx to hell. I guessed that told me one thing, no virgin dies often because we were limited item in the afterlife.

I woke up with a throbbing head. I slept the entire day that I almost forfeited what was left of the afternoon. I was so tired that I didn't even remember how I got back up in my room. All I could remember was the conversation I had back in Olga's chamber. I tried to shake the thought out of my head and considered it as a bad dream but the reality of it clung to my brain and wouldn't let go. When I opened my eyes, I saw the curtain was on the side, no wonder I was covered in blanket because I was cold. I peeled the fabric off my body and sat up. Outside the window the weather was gloomy. It seemed like purgatory felt for what happened last night. I stood up and walked towards the window and leaned over to see the damage outside. I could still see smokes rousing beyond the walls. Though there was no fire, but trees were burned and the groves mourned. Shutters downstairs from all the brick houses were closed and the resident souls of Iduri City were hiding inside. The entire city was intact; the giant wall of Iduri did a great job serving its purpose but for how long? That we didn't know. I looked down to see that I was wearing an oversize shirt and my underwear. My mind was racing with different possibilities and I was hoping and praying that it wasn't Keenan who put me in this fresh sleeping garb. I would kill him if I found out that he was the one who undressed me last night. I turned around to find my Guardian uniform properly pressed on the table with a note on the top.

I read the note and it was from Keenan telling me that Sula put me on the fresh clothes which was a gift from Olga. I sighed with relief thinking that Keenan didn't see me in the state of comatose undressing. Keenan noted that I slept in Olga's chamber and that he carried me upstairs to my room when the first light came. How nice of him to do that. I looked back at the window thinking what would be like outside. I was in purgatory for two days now and I knew that this would be my home for a long time. A crazy idea popped in my head. I decided to get to know the city and had a little exploring. In haste, I changed outfit and put on my Guardian uniform and stormed out of the room. The elevator groaned as it opened. In a minute I found myself outside the main door of Zion Headquarter, ready to take what the City of Iduri had to offer. I looked up and saw that despite of the gloomy weather, the sky was clear; no sign for the rain to come. I turned left and right to see if I could find anyone but there was none. The cobblestone alley was deserted and I was alone standing in front of the Headquarters' building undecided which way to go. I was about to make my first step when I felt a presence behind me. I turned to find Olga standing at the main door watching fondly. She smiled and I returned the gesture slyly like a grounded teenager caught by a parent sneaking out on a Friday evening. She advanced and the more she closed the gap between us, her grin widened.

"Where do you think you're going?" She asked.

"Uhmmm I just wanted to walk around... get to know the place?" I stuttered, waiting for the scold to come from Olga. I was surprised that she didn't reprimand me by my bold action of sneaking out. In fact, she smiled warmly and tagged me in the arm and ushered me to the alleyway as we moved forward.

"I apologize for not able to tour you around. I should have done this earlier but given the situation we are in..." She paused and looked at me. Her stares radiated earnestly that warmed my soul. She faced the road and tagged me along as we walked slowly. "There's no excuse Lola. You deserve to see Iduri; this will be your home for a while." She said.

We emerged in what seemed to be a courtyard. I saw Olive trees and garden with assortment of flowers on the side. There was playground as well but instead of children roaming around, or people chattering in different languages, the courtyard was empty. Olga and I stood at the middle observing. My eyes wandered around brick walls of houses and closed windows. There was a dreadful stillness in the surrounding. I couldn't hear a thing, only the whispers of chilly wind caught my hearing. I shivered and wrapped my arms around me.

"The souls are afraid because of what happened last night. I couldn't blame them because they have the reason to... We all have the reason to be afraid." Olga faced me and I saw sadness in her face. It was crazy to think that a soul like Olga could age in a second. How sadness could change a soul or even a person if you will. I closed the gap between us and unconsciously reached out for her hand to console her. She held my hand tighter and assured me that she was okay. We continued to walk and exited from the courtyard. The marketplace was emptied with traders and vendors as well... The place was supposed to be at the center of Iduri and known to be the most crowded but because of the recent event, the city was ghostlike and looked abandoned. How the attacked shuttered confidence and inflicted fear to a soul was overwhelming and I felt for the souls of Iduri. I didn't want to risk all of them to save myself. It wasn't right; my conscience couldn't handle it. All souls had the right to stand in the mirror of truth and proceed to a higher level in the afterlife. What was the next level anyway? My mind stirred with this question.

The moment we drifted out from the marketplace; I got the chance to ask Olga.

"What is the mirror of truth?" I asked directly.

Olga looked at me and she was amused by my thirst for knowledge. It seemed that she liked my enthusiasm to learn about the whole thing. She cleared her throat and said.

"I'll tell you everything about it but first I want to show you something."

"What?"

"The Temple ofSaint Peter."

Chapter 11

The Temple of Saint Peter was in a very unusual location. From the marketplace, Olga and I entered a shortcut alley that led us to another courtyard. I turned around to have a final view of the deserted marketplace before finding my way and followed Olga in the narrow passage. The courtyard opened with a fountain in the middle. Water flowed in a basin held by a female angel, bending slightly while beautiful wings spread behind her. It was a life-sized statue and judging by her feminine structure and clothing, I assumed it was a female, with a face so regal that would shame the finest gem. I followed Olga as we walked around the statue, yet my eyes were glued on the angel's face. As if where kindness emanated, that was how I described it. I suddenly wondered what it would be like meeting the real thing. What would it be like standing face to face with the real being... an Angel of the Lord? I sighed and moved on as I clung to the thought of meeting a real angel in person. As I looked around, I was bathed with the wonders I saw in the garden. There was an explosion of colors from the different kind of flowers that I've never seen before. It was beautiful! Of course, I recognized those that were available in Idmuria, roses, daises and sunflowers on this side and lilac on the other and there were many other plants that a botanist would kill for. The thing that amazed me was all the flowers that bloomed in the garden were bigger than those in the living world. I was awed and captivated. Olga and I walked beneath the canopy of overlapping tree branches, in the cobbled pathway to the Temple but wherever I looked I marveled at the beauty of the garden that I stumbled several times. There were trees as well, many of them. I assumed that these trees were old as time that some of it arching towards us with branches touching the ground. I saw trees bearing fruit such as apple and oranges, typical right? But there were trees that bore bigger fruits which I wasn't familiar of. Olga glanced on her shoulder and smiled. She was amused of how delighted I was of what I had beheld. I met her gaze and returned her the gesture.

"Is this the Garden of Eden?" I asked.

Olga laughed and slowly shook her head. "No Lola. The Garden of Eden is incomparable, this." She opened her hands referring to the whole wonders around us. "Is nothing. Even the plants of Saint Peter will dim from the radiance that can be seen in Eden." She looked at me and her gaze was thoughtful.

"Why?" I asked eagerly.

"Because it was made by the Supreme Ruler, it was made by God himself." She said it with reverence.

"Oh, but where are we?" I turned around again to see the entire Garden.

"We are at the Rock, The Temple of Saint Peter." She said.

"But I don't see any Temple."

"You have to look deeper. Opened your heart and don't be deceive by what the eyes can see." She finished.

I was confused and I stared at Olga's beautiful face. Opened my heart she said, but how? I knew what I must do. I closed my eyes and filled my mind the joy I felt when I entered the Garden. I was still in the lowest realm, but it seemed that I left Purgatory the moment we passed through the fountain with the angel in the courtyard. I breathed in and smelled the delicate scent of jasmine in the air. I smelled lavender as well and a smile broke in my face while my body relaxed. I filled my heart with joy and remember the feeling I felt when I stood in front of Raphael's statue at the base. As if my heart would burst in hymn with cherubic voices, I let it embrace me.

"Open your eyes Lola." Olga said.

When I opened my eyes, I saw Olga in front of me but what caught my attention was the peculiar structure behind her that wasn't there a minute ago. We were standing at the foot of the temple and in front of me was a huge golden door that was opened, ready to accommodate us. I was hoping to see Saint Peter's Basilica, but this was nothing liked it. The Temple of Saint Peter was more of an auditorium rather than an immense Cathedral that normally depict churches. The entire structure was circular in shape with many windows surrounding it. I thought of a garden chapel my mom and I visited once back in the living world. Despite of how odd it was, the Temple was beautiful. It wasn't the Notre Dame in Paris and it might not have the Byzantine or the Baroque style of the Basilicas, but this temple was the real thing.

"It might not be the one that you expected but this is the Temple of Saint Peter. The Rock, as we normally call it at the base." Olga explained, still facing me.

"It was beautiful." I said. "I've never been to a Temple before so... I really don't know what to expect." I chuckled and smirked at Olga who was still studying me.

"Look! The door is open... Someone must be inside."

For a second, I saw Olga's reaction changed from serene to alarm. I didn't know what part of what I said triggered it, but I suddenly realized that the door of the Temple should be close all the time and seeing it opened meant that something was not right. She turned around and entered the Temple in haste, leaving me perplexed. I followed behind trying to catch her pace. Olga stopped and gasped in shock; her body tensed. She must have seen something that knocked the air out of her. I quickened my pace to see what it was, but I wasn't prepared for what awaited me inside the Temple. When I reached her, I was out of breath, I almost stumbled but found my footing right away.

Inside, the Temple was spacious; all the windows surrounding it were opened to accommodate the air. I smelled incense and perfume everywhere probably from all the candles on each side near the wall. Other than candles there was a pool at the center filled with clear water, it must be from a divine spring it fount for its crystal clearness mirrored your reflection. So, the Mirror of Truth was not really an actual mirror, it was a water - a fountain of truth. But what painted horror from Olga was not the solemnity that greeted us inside but the one lying face down beside the pool. It was a body of a man in a white robe, unconscious. I suddenly held my breath when I saw the man, was he dead? That was a silly question, given the fact that we were all dead here. My eyes pointed to Olga who was looking morosely at the forsaken being. She was motionless, shocked by the terror she beheld. I called her name and in an instant, she was back again as if she just woke up from a nightmarish dream. She moved forward hasting and reached for the fallen man and turned him to face her. The man was still alive yet battered and bruised all over his face. He was old and wrinkled but his eyes were bright and blue like the sky during summer when he opened it to look at Olga. She tried to pull him up, but the man groaned in pain and Olga decided to lay him still.

"Sound the bell, call the others hurry!" She ordered me.

I panicked and turned around to find the bell that Olga wanted me to sound to alert the other Guardians. There was no bell inside the Temple. Where did they keep the damn bell? Then I remember, all bells in cathedral were placed at the top to call for church goers before the mass started. I turned and ran to the exit; the bell must be outside. When I reached the main door, I covered all places and finally there it was. I found it! It was situated on the left side of the Temple, hung a few inches from the ground. The Temple bell was made of gold, huge and shiny. I ran towards it, surging through the cobbled pathway to where it was located. When I finally reached the bell, I didn't waste much time and held the rope hanging on the side. I thought about the man dying on the floor with Olga. I needed to call the guardians for help. I knew how this works because I've seen this done by Altar boys at Saint Augustine Parish. With all the strength I could master, I closed my eyes and pulled the rope as much as I could, and it worked. The bell sounded and it wasn't the normal sound I heard from churches. For starter, it didn't sound like a bell at all. My eardrums didn't explode given how huge the bell was and how close I was to it. The ethereal sound scattered on the surrounding like thousand trumpets blown at once. It hummed in the air and the volume became louder as the sound travelled farther from its source. The birds flew from the branches; the animals hid on their lair while the trees and plants went still as the bell rang. The muscles in my forearms swelled and I was losing my grip on the rope, but I held on to it. When I thought that the bell had rung enough, I stopped and the sound coming from the bell also ceased. I breathed heavily; I was spent. It seemed that all the oxygen in my small body was pumped out. Instinctively I filled my lungs with fresh air until my breathing was back to normal. I thought about Olga and the dying man inside the Temple and immediately I started moving towards the entrance door. Halfway through the door, I saw movement far ahead. Then from the branches of the trees the Guardians emerged. They arrived all at once, emerging from the trees while others running on the cobbled pathway. I recognized Keenan right away, weaving through the crowd of Guardians mustered in front of the Temple. It seemed everybody was here, clad in battle attire ready for the threat. I saw Sula as she walked to the front. I stood in front of them looking sheepishly and small. Sula approached me and held my arm. Her grip was tight, but I didn't flinch.

"What's wrong? Why did you sound the alarm? The bell has not been used for thousands of years." She said angrily.

"Sula..." It was Keenan stepping forward.

"I asked her to do it." Olga said loudly. She was standing at the foot of the church. Her eyes damped from crying, her face was grave and sad.

Everybody turned to face her, even Sula. I turned to face her, and I saw her bare hands turned into a fist.

"The Temple has been attacked." She started, trying to put strength in her voice. "The Prier ascended to the fifth realm. He perished in my arms a minute ago. We were too late." She swallowed.

I heard gasped from the guardians; everybody was shocked. They looked at each other in horror and their eyes settled back on the front asking question. No one made a sound, they were contemplating and confused. I heard the wind whispered in silence, I felt the leaves started to sway from the trees then Sula walked slowly towards Olga and spoke.

"There's a traitor in our midst. No high or low born Darklings could penetrate Saint Peter's Temple unless the person responsible is already inside the walls." She spun around and faced the troubled Guardians. "Whoever did this; is a Guardian gone rogue. Whoever that is, has chosen to side the darkness." Her words heeded with warning. "Whoever that soul is? Is a traitor to the realm and we will search every swamp and woodland to find and judge the quisling scum!" She yelled and the Guardians broke a deafening roar of agreement. I found Keenan watching me with a mischievous smile on his lips. He nodded and joined the uproar and chants of the Guardians.

Chapter 12

"Jabaree!" Keenan spoke when the uproar subsided. A small skin head Asian guy who looked like a monk stepped forward to the front line and faced Keenan. "Go to the Mission and inform the Priests and Nuns of what happened here..." He stopped and looked at Olga who was still standing at the foot of the Temple. "Tell them the untimely ascension of the Prier..." The guy named Jabaree bowed, turned around and disappeared in the crowd. I looked at Keenan whose face looked serious all of a sudden. "We need to lockdown the Temple. We cannot let any soul be judge until the Mission voted a new Prier.

"Keenan, there would be chaos in the Purgatory." Sula said. Her eyes darted from Keenan to Olga who was still looking forlorn for what happened.

"Don't you think I know that Sula? We don't have a choice. Only a chosen Prier has the privilege to make the Mirror of Truth works. Without the Prier, the mirror will not answer to anyone of us. You know this." There was a weight on Keenan's voice and Sula bowed her head to acknowledge the truth in his brother's words.

"But what about the souls." She whispered.

"We will deal with them." Olga said finally. "We cannot afford panic in the realm so whoever did this... needs to be found."

The sky burned red when we reached the marketplace on our way back to Zion. The main street and alleyways were still deserted but I saw shutters opened in several bricked houses we came across on our way to the headquarter. Candle lights flickered in every home as darkness crept around the city heralding the night. I imagined souls gathered around table having dinner. As we were walking on the main cobbled road, I took a glance at the enormous walls eerily presaging a sinister vibes. These huge walls that stood for eons were the citadels guarding the city were now failing. What would happen to the souls of Iduri if the enemies continued to sneak inside under the Guardians noses?

A presence distracted me and I felt Keenan's heavy breathing on my side. He slowdown his stride to match mine and I brought myself to look at him. His pale skin made him looked like a ghost in the night but this was normal to most of us souls here at Purgatory. His eyes were distant, looking far ahead at nothing, strands of black hair fell threatening to cover his eyes but he didn't do anything to brush it aside. His mind drifted far from which I couldn't follow. His head tilted up making the fine jawline visible outlining his beautiful face. I didn't want to bother him and pulled him out of his musing and so I kept my silence and faced forward. I diverted my mind to something else, trying to find something attention worthy. But Keenan walking beside me made it harder to focus to anything in my surrounding other than him. His presence was overbearing, determined not to be ignore. Now that he sealed my attention only for him, all I could do was to listen to him walk beside me, his every footfall, even the swaying of his hands on his side and his graceful stride.

"You did great." He finally said. His voice husky and low trying to break the silence between us. When I looked at him, his face was still tilted up facing the front. He didn't even bother to look down at me. What's wrong with this guy? I thought.

"Err thanks?" I mumbled.

Then there was that irritating silence once again. My eyes wondered forcing to distract myself from this brood male figure at my side. Dusk was already upon us and the last light disappeared as darkness swallowed the entire realm. Fire danced from the lamps while shadows moved from the walls.

"I was just thinking." I started. "Thinking about what?" Keenan answered right away.

"We are souls right?" I asked.

"Yes, the last time I check." He said suddenly mocking.

I chuckled, relieved that the tension melted and Keenan recovered from his musing.

"Okay, so we are souls, technically we are dead...What happens if we perish unexpectedly, without being judge? Do we ascend to the higher realm too?" I asked.

Keenan didn't answer right away. I felt that he was solemnly contemplating about my question, doing his best to provide the accurate answer. It might not be the one that I wanted to hear but it was the truth. He sighed heavily and said.

"We are dead in Idmuria Lola. Our physical body died there and we are no longer bound to that world. But here in Iduri, in Purgatory, we are much alive as we were once alive in the world of the living." He paused and I managed to take a glance at his direction to see why. His brows furrowed thinking. "Only the Prier and the Mission Priests and Nuns have the privilege to ascend without facing the Mirror or Truth."

"How about us? What happen to us if...?" My voice went up a notch indicating the panic that I felt.

"We vanish in oblivion." His voice fell into a whisper.

"But that doesn't make any sense... that is absurd!" I swallowed the tears; my voice was breaking the next time I spoke.

"That's not fair! We couldn't just vanish!" I was afraid and the fear reflected in my face. I couldn't just die and stop existing. It was worst dying in Purgatory than on Earth. Imagine being totally erased, as if you never existed at all which was worse than death or any catastrophic event ever existed. Keenan stopped walking and turned to face me, his reaction was serious as he looked at me straight in the eye.

"It's not all about being fair Lola. It's just how it is and there's nothing you can do about it but to accept it. That's the fact and the earlier you accept what's true, the better." He said.

Keenan turned around and walked ahead of me, leaving me standing thinking gravely about what he said. Maybe he was right, maybe

I should start accepting that I died and now this was my new reality and that no matter how I detested the truth, it would just make harder for me to move on if I refused to embrace it. I didn't want to be known as the girl who just wept in the corner unable to move forward. I wanted to be better than that, I wanted to be stronger. I wanted to embrace the new life given to me and lived day by day until my time came to face the Mirror of Truth. I wanted to take this challenge and the first thing I wanted to do was to accept the Guardianship that Olga offered. Then I wanted to train how to defend myself to avoid being killed. If the leader of the Darklings wanted me then he would try again to attack the city and if by chance I would come face to face with him again, I would make sure that I wasn't the girl that he saw the first time he laid eyes on me. I didn't know if I could develop skills in combat but I would protect myself the best way that I could. I watched Keenan's back disappeared into the night and far ahead the Zion Headquarter stood in utter stillness. The old building was illuminated with two huge torches situated parallel from each other at the entrance. A smile formed in my lips as I walked slowly towards Zion. I wanted to be a Guardian.

Chapter 13

The ray of the sun bled from the opening in my window. My somehow worn-out curtain had been slightly moved by the wind. I overslept. Immediately, I sat up only to hold still on the edge of my bed. My head felt heavy for the long hours of sleep, my body was no longer accustomed to it. I closed my eyes allowing for the dizziness to pass. After a few minutes, my vision was back to normal and the room was no longer turning, I stood. The light outside bathed my room and the last remnant of the dream world slowly disintegrated until the sun claimed the entire city. I walked a few steps and reached for my Guardian uniform and put it on. I went to the small lavatory in my room and washed my face. As I leaned back, I had a glimpse of myself in a remnant of a shattered mirror on the wall. My face was gaunt, my cheeks sunken as if I aged tremendously since I got here but it was still me. My reflection stared at me as I combed my hair using my hands and took a small rubber band hair I found in a small medicine cabinet plastered on the wall and seamlessly tied my hair in a knot. For the last time I looked at myself in the mirror, probably the dark shades around my eyes were permanent but that I didn't know for sure. The freckles were no longer there but my light green eyes blazed with so much life. I stormed out from the room hasting, heading down to the base.

The elevator door creaked as it opened and I moved out and walked on the mighty angel hallway to the cafeteria. I offered a small prayer to the Archangel when I walked passed his statue at the end before I turned to another hallway where the cafeteria was located. Inside the medieval canteen, everybody was eating. The long tables were occupied except the ones at the back. Some of the Guardians looked up and nodded at my direction and I gave them a shy smile in acknowledgement. I bowed my head trying to look small to avoid catching any attention. Walking toward the buffet table took forever but I made every step count silently. Finally I made it and the sight of the food prepared on the table was delightful to look at that even the saddest soul would be uplifted. My stomach rambled as I let my tongue out and ran it on my lips. A guy with a dark hair offered a plate and I immediately took it and said my thanks. He nodded and turned away. I wasn't fond of eating meat but because of how hungry I was, I took a filleted fish and a bunch of green vegies on the side. The pastry couldn't escape the preying of my hungry eyes. I took three cupcakes, the red velvet, one lemon and a blueberry. My eyes danced as I watched the stuff I put on my plate, these food would last a lifetime of eating but I didn't care, I was hungry. I turned around eyeing the empty table on the far back but I heard a tingling voice called my name. I turned to see who it was, Safa. I smiled and walked to where she sat and placed my food on the table in front of her. When I settled I saw Safa smiling at me.

"What?" I said.

"Can you eat all that?" She said teasing.

"I'm hungry! I'm so hungry I could eat a horse." I said.

"You can't! That's too big and..." She was horrified.

"Safa, I'm just joking..."

"Oh..."

I felt sorry for Safa that in her innocence, she must be dead for a long time that she forgot how it was to loosen up a bit. The girl couldn't take a joke, she took everything seriously. Safa mirrored most of the souls here in Iduri, uptight and tensed. How could a person live that way? Right, we're already dead, what was the worst thing that could happen? Then I remembered what Keenan said. We vanish in oblivion - I would not let that happen to me or to Safa.

We ate silently. Safa was busy with her beans and I was enjoying what's left of my cupcake. She stood up to get us drinks and returned with two glasses of lemonade. I thanked her and she smiled at me. A moment later, a bell rang at the front for attention and all of us along with other Guardians turned to face who it was. Olga stood at the front wearing a white silky gown. She looked beautiful in it. Her red hair was tied loosely on her back. On her side there were others. An older man wearing a white robe stood solemnly observing, next to him was a woman standing meekly while hands clamped together in prayer in front of her. She was smaller than Olga but quite older too. The two visitors looked serene and holy but obviously they'd suffered grief and loss from the unexpected ascension of the revered Prier.

"The holies of The Mission." Safa said.

"What?" I inquired.

"They're the nun and priest from The Mission... representative I mean" Said Safa.

"What are they doing here?"

She shrugged, a way of telling me that she didn't have a clue.

The entrance door opened and Keenan bolted in followed by Jabaree the Asian monk. Safa and I snaked our way into the front and we stood next to Sula whose face was somehow contorted with anger. This wasn't new with Sula since she was always angry at anything. Olga cleared her throat and spoke. Though unsettledness stricken her due to the current events, she managed to speak evenly and direct.

"Guardians, the holies of The Mission are here to deliver a message. I'm afraid to tell you that a new Prier is yet to be decided for we have an urgent concern that needs to be address immediately." I heard murmurs from the crowd and Safa and I exchanged nervous glances while Sula stood quietly still. Olga turned her attention toward the priest and gave him a slight nod; a sign for him to start talking now that Olga captured everybody's attention. The priest stepped forward but he stayed in silence until the murmurs turned to hum and then died down. Everybody was holding their breath, waiting for the priest to deliver his news. As he stood in front of us, I noticed his calm demeanor as he surveyed every face in the crowd and despite of how old he was, I saw kindness behind the lines in his face. But his eyes, just liked the Prier who died, blazed in brilliant blue. The nun who stood behind mirrored the same distinction as the Priest. They were the complete contradiction of the restless Guardians who were currently on the edge of their emotion. Sula was a ticking bomb beside me and I was afraid to disrupt her. Desperation could make humans do silly things, perhaps souls were no different. Fear or even anger could steal the reason that might push her to start a war against the enemy without considering the rationale. The entire cafeteria went silent and I could feel the contained agitation from all the Guardians while waiting for the priest to say his piece. I turned my head to see clenched jaws while hands turned to fist and unsteady eyes. This was the Guardians giving way to patience, as if rage barred in a cage. It was even ridiculous to look at but I snapped out of it. I was ashamed of what I did. Who was I to judge them - my now brothers and sisters? I turned my attention back to the figure at the front. Finally the priest spoke.

"My name is Father Valiant of The Mission. I am a priest of the first order of the light and with me is Sister Socorro. She is a nun of the first order of the light as well." Sister Socorro bowed her head as the priest introduced her. The Holies were quite a spectacles to behold, I could imagine wings expanding behind their back but they were no angels, but guardians of the Temple and overseers of souls. The Holies mission was to guide souls so they could step to the next level in the afterlife. It's part of their responsibility to equip the souls with knowledge before crossing the Everlasting River.

"But how did they become the Holies?" I asked Safa quietly.

"They were exceptional servants of the Lord when they were still in Idmuria." Safa whispered.

"You mean when they were still alive?"

"If that's what you prefer." She shrugged.

Father Valiant continued. His voice was calm and comforting, helping the tension to ease up a bit. But that didn't do much because the message that the Holies brought created a perfect pandemonium inside the cafeteria that even Keenan stepped forward to establish decorum to the raging Guardians.

"Father Benedict was truly revered by every soul in our city and his untimely ascension was a shocking revelation that even the Holies of the Mission scrambled in darkness, seeking for reasons of why and how this happened." He breathed, taking his time, choosing the right words to address the crowd. "The Rock, is one of the most hallowed grounds in Purgatory and I believed that by now we are all convinced that whoever did this is a traitor living among us. We have to be vigilant and cautious in every move that we make because the entire city is no longer safe. We didn't know how many of them who have chosen to side with the enemy."

I turned around to see worried faces glancing at each other, murmurs began to rise like buzzing bees. Sula shifted and I saw her looked at Keenan. Their eyes locked for a short period of time as if tied in a telepathic conversation. For a moment nobody speak a word and the Holies at the front stood facing the crowd observing the muttering. Something told me that there was something the Holies not telling us, that what the priest told us was just the tip of the iceberg and there was more to it, more devastating news and I braced myself.

From the corner I saw Sister Socorro stepped forward and the noises mellowed until everyone from the crowd stopped talking and faced the front in silence.

"Guardians!" She started, her voice was as commanding as Olga. "There's no other way to tell you this that would not set your alarm." She paused and her brilliant blue eyes surveyed the surrounding until it settled on me. I shivered as her gaze penetrated my soul making me numbed inside. But I didn't back down, I didn't bow my head to sever the contact. I clenched my jaw and narrowed my gaze as I stared back.

"The revered Prier died defending something, something that is more valuable not only for us souls living in the city but for the city itself. The healing salve of the Archangel Rafael has been stolen and Father Benedict fought very hard to defend the salve that resulted for his untimely ascension." She paused and the graved news she released sent an overwhelming shock that gave way to unspeakable silence in the crowd.

"The Holies of the Mission are trained fighters and we strongly believe that Father Ben battled the enemy until he could no longer fight. Whoever the traitor is, got what he or she came for..." Chaos irrupted among the Guardians. There were those who were scared and worried but most of them reflected rage and anger. A big guy with a dirty blonde hair wanted to plot an attack to the enemy and others agreed to him but there were those who opposed and saw reason instead. With all of this, Keenan stood still watching the Guardians interacted. Beside him was the Asian monk Jabaree who somehow confused.

"What happen to the city now without the salve?" Sula could no longer restrain herself. She stepped forward with eyes blaring. Olga moved toward her and wrapped an arm around her, easing her. I looked at Sister Socorro again, waiting for her to answer the question Sula threw. Everybody was holding their breath.

"The healing salve purifies the souls after they face the Mirror of Truth. Without it no one can cross the Everlasting River and all souls we'll be stuck here in Purgatory." She said.

"The salve is a powerful weapon." It was Father Valiant who spoke. "It can heal almost anything. No physical illness will not yield to the power of the healing salve. It could not only heal the physical body but even the world from all its chaos and suffering." He inhaled. "But if the salve falls under the wrong hands then instead of healing the world, it can destroy it."

"The end of the world." I said. I was staring at Father Valiant, submerged in the thought of Armageddon if the salve fell to the enemies. I didn't realize that I mumbled the words out loud and now everybody was staring at me. I looked down embarrassed.

"Lola is right." It was Olga who spoke. "The Holies are convinced that whoever took the salve found a way to cross the portal back to Idmuria. Whoever the traitor is, wants to use the salve to destroy the world of the living. If that happen, millions of people will die and

Iduri City will be flooded with souls who can't ascend to the next level. Both worlds are facing its doom."

"But we are souls!" Someone shouted from the crowd. "We don't exist in Idmuria, we don't have a physical body there." The guy said and everybody agreed with him.

"My dear ones, you must have forgotten that this is the healing salve of the Archangel Raphael. Whoever hold the salve in his possession can do anything." Answered Sister Socorro.

The cafeteria burst into chaos. Everyone was shouting and throwing their opinions in the air, some were asking what we should do. In the midst of all this, my mind was racing with all the possibilities the event presented. I could go back to Idmuria, to the living world, to Earth and lived again. But I felt bad for my own selfish reason and I pushed the thought down at the back of my head. A smile formed in my lips as I thought about seeing my family again.

And for the first time, there was hope.

Chapter 14

There was a knock on my door around mid-afternoon. I was literally dawdling on my bed thinking about what the Holies told us this morning at the cafeteria. I got up and opened the door thinking it was probably Safa. But I was greeted with a sight of Keenan standing in front of me.

"Hey." He said.

"Hey." My heart was up my throat. Keenan must be so stressed out with what was happening inside the Iduri walls. I could almost feel the pressure that the situation brought to everyone, especially to the Guardians and Keenan wasn't an exception to it. But as he stood in front of my door waiting for me to invite him in, all I saw was the dark haired boy, weary with black eyes peering on me. His lips parted, wet and delicious. What a mess, what a beautiful mess he was.

"Lola, are you okay?" He asked and my face burned with embarrassment knowing that he caught me subdued by his presence. I turned around immediately as I invited him in. I heard the door closed but I didn't turn to face him right away. Instead, I crossed the room and stood in front of the window looking at the walls outside. Dark and malevolent billow clustered on the horizon – a storm was coming.

"Lola?" He asked for the second time.

I sucked in air and finally faced Keenan. I saw the concern written all over his face as I looked at him trying to hide the blushing. "Sorry, I'm just thinking about what the Holies said..." I lied.

He nodded and walked slowly toward me. I suddenly had the urged to fidget but I stopped myself. I know, hard habit was hard to break but I bit the inside of my lips to stop myself from looking like a stupid girl in front of Keenan.

"I know what you mean. I was thinking about it too, in fact every-one was thinking about it." He said.

He was now standing in front of me, his broad shoulders blocking the door. With his tall figure, my gaze leveled to his chest and so I tilted my head to distract myself, uncomfortably looking at a space on the side. He was peering down at me, I could feel his watchful eyes warmed my skin. I looked up to see his face. Our eyes met and for the first time I saw Keenan through the mirror in his eyes. There was a cliché that the eyes were the windows to the soul – now I could attest that there was truth in those words. Keenan was beyond exhaustion and I could see a tiny flickered in his soul, the only thing that kept him from fainting.

"When was the last time you sleep?" I asked.

"It doesn't matter." He said breaking the contact.

"You're exhausted Keenan. You need to rest." I retorted following his gaze. I would never back down on this. Keenan needed to regain his strength.

"Nonsense! We need to..." I didn't allow him to finish his rebuttal and immediately I reached out for his face and guided it to face me.

"I'm fine Lola." He was still trying to play hard but I wasn't having it. I knew what I saw and I knew that he was already at the edge.

"You can't save the city if you yourself needed saving. Come..." I held his hand and pulled him towards the bed.

"I need to go back to the base..." He was so stubborn.

"Lie down with me..." I asked him. I couldn't imagine myself to be this daring. I've never done this before, lying in bed with a man at my side but if it was the only way for Keenan to listen then be it. Keenan stopped talking and all he did was stare at me and I held his gaze. I could feel my heart fluttered like wings and a burning sensation surged inside my body as Keenan leaned forward to share my bed. I lied down next to the wall as he rolled in his side facing me.

"What are you doing to me?" He asked. "I wanted to say no but I couldn't."

"I just wanted you to rest for a while Keenan, if you're going to save the city – you'll be needing your strength." I reached out for his face and placed a hand to caress him. My body was trembling with this boldness. Our faces were inch from each other that I could even feel the warmth of his breathe. I've never been close like this with Keenan, not this close.

"Sleep now." I whispered.

He was fighting the fatigue but tiredness ruled over him and finally he surrendered, his eyes closed yielding to the dream. But before the strong of his will gave up he spoke.

"I like you Lola."

Chapter 15

A whooshing sound woke me up. The temperature of the room drastically decreased, signifying that it was already night time. I reached out on my side to see if Keenan was still asleep but I was disappointed to know that my hand touched the hollowed space on my bed that he had long vacated. I could no longer feel the warmth essence of his body on my pillow, giving me an estimation that he had left probably an hour before I woke. I opened my eyes and found the room illuminated by two huge candles neatly placed on the side table. I wanted to be mad at him for not waking me before he left but I held back... at least he didn't leave me scrambling in the dark – how thoughtful of him.

I sat up and my eyes darted immediately to the window. I remembered the sound that woke me and it felt as if someone in the room watching while I was asleep. I stood hasting and moved slowly, tiptoeing toward the window thinking that I might caught someone sneaking. Only the wind moaned as it splashed on the building's wall, other than that, there was no one in there.

The feeling of someone watching hung in the air and I knew that there was something off. My eyes surveyed the surrounding but all I saw was the silhouette of roofs and the city walls against the darkness. It was quiet outside, the kind of stillness before a giant tsunami hit the shore. But it was probably nothing. I must have imagined it or it must be the absence of Keenan that made me agitated. But there was that off feeling that I couldn't pin point. Odd as it may seemed, the air inside the room changed. I could smell gas that came out of nowhere and in minute I was beginning to suffocate. I knew this smell as I smelled this before. Suddenly my heart pounded like hooves in my chest. I knew that there was something wrong and before I could turn and ran to the door, a gasp of wind blew the flickers from the candles in the room. Darkness flooded and I could see nothing. Wherever I turned I was blinded. I stayed motionless as panic surged in my veins. I felt my heart was going to explode. Then I heard an eerie sound that made all the hair of my body stood. As if tiny metals scraping the walls of my room, producing a shrieking noise that made even a rodent cringed. I turned around following the sound but it was everywhere and my knees buckled with fear, amounting myself to pull down to the ground, crouching with my hands covering my ears. The sound stopped and silence stretched the time. All I could hear was the drumming of my heart behind my ears.

"Lola." A male's voice – as if it was spoken underground with its sound bouncing on the walls.

I turned around to follow the location of the voice but my eyes were concealed in complete darkness. The smell of gas invaded my nostril and it got stronger by the minute that I had to cover my nose and breathed through my mouth. The temperature inside became totally cold that I was literally shivering on the ground with my arms wrapped around myself. I was waiting for the final blow, for annihilation to come and embraced nothingness. I remembered what Keenan said about not having a chance of ascending to the next realm – so after this I would just vanish. I braced for myself. I waited and the longer it got the more it became unbearable.

"Go ahead! Kill me!" I shouted. My voice was trembling.

All of a sudden a flicker appeared in front of me against the dark. I held my breath as I watched the flame dance back and forth. Where did it come from? There was no candle, just a flame suspended in the air. Then a figure from the darkness began to appear while the light from the flicker in front of the figure illuminated it sent an unspeakable horror. As the figure came closer my body shivered while my nails sunk inside my palm as I made a fist. It was the figure of my father gawking at me from the flicker. I stared at it in horror. This was the devil taking many forms. I knew this because I knew about the devil from the scriptures I read. The devil, master of tricks and deception, the ultimate con artist that would do any ruse to send people to the edge and shattered their humanity. I would not fall for it because I knew that this wasn't true but then the figure of my father spoke that sent the tears falling from my eyes. It also got my father's voice – his loving voice. How could I not fall for it? This darkling was so good that it made me believe that it was really my father I was seeing.

"Lola." Said the image of my father. "I miss you so much my dear."

"Dad?" I cried. "Oh daddy, I miss you too..." I was that girl again. The girl with my brother Ram who waited every weekend for my father's visit.

"Come with me Lola. Let's go home. I need you." The image said.

I was sobbing and I couldn't control the tears. I missed him so much, my father. Seeing him standing in front of me made me missed him even more. I wanted to run toward him and just be in his arms and everything would be okay. Just like the old times, when I was a little girl. But this wasn't the old time and I was no longer the little girl who was vulnerable and naïve. I knew this was a trick.

"You're not my father!" I yelled at the figure. "Stay away from me!" My eyes were clouded with tears and I blinked.

The figure flickered behind the flame and the next time I looked, the figure changed. My heart beats liked wings in a cage and I brought both of my hands at my chest to contain myself. It was my mother staring at me and calling my name. I cried hard as my very soul shattered. The darkling would never stop until there was nothing left in me but a broken soul. I shuddered hard and I screamed. My mother disappeared and replaced by the image of my brother Ram but this time it was different. My brother's eyes were distantly staring while blood dripping from the slit in his throat. I wailed violently in all four with palms flat on the floor. I couldn't look at it any more. The sight of my brother dead was too much to take. Then I heard a familiar voice calling my name that made me looked up.

The wavy blonde hair that was almost golden when hit by the ray of sun, the beautiful face with lips slightly opened and those eyes, bright blue as if holding the entire sky.

"Seb." I whispered.

I handed it to the darkling the artistry of the craft. It was really Sebastian Whyte who was standing behind the flame. Even the way his mouth moved when he spoke, the way he arched his brow and the way he stared at me. If I didn't know better, I would have flung myself toward the image.

"Lola." Seb's image whispered and I closed my eyes to savor the timbre of his voice calling my name. But I knew this wasn't Seb. The real Seb was alive at Idmuria and I was the one who was dead. I had to find my strength to get through with this... The demon would never stop until I gave in to what it wanted of me.

"Stop!" I yelled but the image of Seb was still calling my name. I drew the last strength in my heart, the one that I could muster to fight this madness. I would not give in and I would rather vanish in oblivion than succumb.

"This isn't real." I told myself. "Tricks. These are all tricks." I kept repeating it in my head with my eyes closed. I didn't notice that I was bellowing the word Tricks louder like a mantra. As the minute passed the demon's voice was moving farther away as if it was at the other end of the tunnel. Then a loud blow somewhere on the wall. I covered myself as I scrambled to the ground shivering. Lights flooded my room accompanied with voices I didn't recognize. The voices were calling my name and I wasn't sure if this was still one of the darkling's tricks so I kept covering my face. Then a hand touched me as if someone pressed a button inside my body that triggered for me to scream louder. The hands gripped my shoulders and gently shaking me.

"Lola, it's me." The voice said. "It's me. You're okay now."

I knew that voice and for the first time I felt safe with the hands holding me firmly. Never letting me go. The warmed touch of this masculine hands comforted me, telling me that it was okay and that I could relax now. I opened my eyes and those set of dark eyes met my gaze.

"Keenan."

Chapter 16

The next time I opened my eyes, I was in a huge bed properly tucked. I moved my head from left to right trying to get a better view of where I was. I recognized this room. I was hoping that it was Keenan's room but it was Olgas. Keenan, where was he? I moved my head again to look for him but it seemed I was alone in the room. Huge candles burned on the walls and there were small ones on the side table held by an ornate gold candelabrum. I stared at it for a second trying to recall what happened. Little by little the memories came back and I remembered. The images of my family and Seb flashed the way the darkling portrayed them. It took all my strength not to scream but I managed to make a noise that sent Olga and Safa rushing by my side.

"Lola." It was the tiny voice of Safa that brought me back to my senses.

"She's still in shock." Olga said. "You need to go back to bed Lola." I could see the concern in her face. I realized that I was already sitting up. She knew how cruelled the Darklings were and to be a victim of their desire was living a life with torment. I saw documentaries when I was still alive and I pitied those people tormented by demons because it brought them death if not a life of nightmarish hell. I lay back in bed and I held Safa's hand as she reached out to comfort me. Olga stood, she was furious about the incident.

"The city is no longer safe." She finally said. Her voice was hard as she accepted the truth. "Since the salve was stolen, the power of the Archangel is failing." She turned around to face Safa who was sitting on the edge of the bed with eyes huge with fear and me watching her carefully. "Without the salve of the Archangel, the city is unprotected. What happened to you Lola will not be the last, we expect more to come and we cannot prevent this from happening." Her eyes were set at nothing but I saw anger in her face. "Hell will rise against us, they will burn this city to the ground until they collected all the souls."

"Why did they want the city so much? Why could they just leave us alone?" I asked.

Olga's eyes met mine and suddenly I saw her face soften. "My dear, the city of Iduri is the only resistant force against the dark realm."

"You mean Hell?" I interrupted.

"Yes. Hell." Olga continued. "The entire Purgatory, the lowest realm of the afterlife is basically a battle ground for recent souls that crossed over from the living world. Without the walls of Iduri, there will be no shelter for them. Hell will claim them the moment they arrived. There are those that are brave enough to fight but not everybody can battle powerful demons. We need to get the salve back."

Safa and I looked at each other and then to Olga whose face was hard contemplating. If what she said was true that the salve was the one protecting the city and now without it the city of Iduri lay defenseless and vulnerable then someone had to make the plan on how to get it back right away. But the healing salve was not here and the one who stole it found a way to cross the portal. I remembered Olga said that and the Holies were convinced that the conniving thief was already in...

"But how?" I was surprised with my eagerness. "How can we get it back if the salve was no longer in the realm? You all said it. We are souls, how can we cross over to Idmuria without the salve?"

Safa's huge eyes were telling me that she also wanted to know. We were waiting for Olga to answer the question. She crossed the room nonchalantly then stopped and immediately faced us. Her eyes fired up as if an idea came to her then her face relaxed as she spoke.

"There is another way to crossover back to the living world." She said. My heart suddenly leaped as she said it. Crossing over back to the living world? That only meant one thing - I would be able to see my family again, my friends and... I shook my head slightly to focus. How could I think of myself when all the souls in Purgatory were in danger and the city was threatened? But the thief was in Idmuria and if the assumption was correct that whoever took it wanted to use it to destroy the world then all the people that I cared for were in grave danger. The thought of it was astounding. We couldn't allow that happen, I couldn't.

"How? How are we going to get the salve back?" It was Safa's high pitched voice disrupted me.

"Call Keenan, Sula and the other leaders. Tell them that I wanted to meet them in my office immediately." She told Safa who responded right away. She patted my hand and smiled slyly as if asking for the permission to leave. I smiled back and slowly squeezed her hand telling her that it was okay. Reassuring her that I would be fine. She bolted out of the room to inform the leaders.

Olga walked towards the bed and sat on my side. Her red long hair flowing behind her back beautifully. Her emerald green eyes glint against her pale face. She was beyond striking, her beauty. As the goddess of the Nile in ancient Egypt. What was her name? Isis? Yes, that's how oddly gorgeous she was.

"How are you feeling?" She asked. Her hand reached out for my face. "I'm okay." I said. But she must had notice the resonance of my voice. I wanted to tell her that the demon almost succeeded. For whatever it did to me, it almost succeeded in breaking me entirely. Whatever was holding me intact right now was doing its job perfectly and I was grateful. I bowed my head and stared at my hands.

"You're strong Lola. No souls will survive torture the way you do. Just believe on the strength that you have. Don't doubt it for an instant." Olga put a hand on top of mine.

We huddled in Olga's bed quietly for a while. She was sitting next to me, holding my hand, caressing it as if she was my mother. But she looked young to be my mother, she was more of a big sister to me. Silence comforted us in that very moment and relished every second of it. I was telling my heart to be still and believed that everything would be fine no matter what. Later on we were distracted with footsteps coming in. I heard many footsteps hasting toward the room.

Olga stood up and smiled at me gingerly. She was slightly annoyed by the interruption but something was telling me that she didn't have a choice. After all she was the leader. The Lady of Zion Headquarter.

As she stood and flattened her dress with her hands, the door of her room opened and Guardian leaders bolted in to answer her summoned. Among them, Keenan walked solemnly to the front. I saw him right away and I caught his eyes the moment he appeared. His face was serious but when he realized that my gaze didn't falter, holding him and never letting him go, his reaction softened and I could see smile coiling in the tip of his mouth. I smiled back and my face flushed when out of nowhere Keenan winked.